Black Reign

Reign & Na'Tae

ERNEST MORRIS

GOOD2GO PUBLISHING

BLACK REIGN
Written by ERNEST MORRIS
Cover Design: Davida Baldwin
Typesetter: Mychea
ISBN: 9781947340107
Copyright ©2017 Good2Go Publishing
Published 2017 by Good2Go Publishing
7311 W. Glass Lane • Laveen, AZ 85339
www.good2gopublishing.com
https://twitter.com/good2gobooks
G2G@good2gopublishing.com
www.facebook.com/good2gopublishing
www.instagram.com/good2gopublishing

Black
Reign

One

"WHEN I'M GETTING MY sneakers back? My mom just brought those jawns, and you had them for weeks now," Wayne asked his homie Trigg as they walked home from school.

"Damn, nigga, my mom's going to the Salvation Army today to pick up some clothes and shoes for me and my sister. Fall back, bro. Just let me rock them until she comes back. Then I'll bring them to you. You act like I'ma fuck them up or something," Trigg replied as they continued on their journey.

"I'm just saying, Tiriq, she's starting to bitch about me letting people hold my new shit that she paid for and I'm not wearing. She thinks I'm wasting her bread, feel me?" Wayne said.

"Oh, believe me; she got her money's worth because these jawns are crazy, bro. Real shit! They comfortable as hell too," Trigg said, knowing he would get a reaction out of him.

"Oh, so you just gonna throw it in my face, knowing damn well that I never even had the chance to step my foot in them jawns. You're lucky you my man, otherwise I would fuck you up," Wayne said, laughing, trying to play it off.

"I'm your big bro. You only twelve years old, which means I have you by three years. I'll beat your ass, lil nigga," Trigg said, grabbing Wayne and putting him in a headlock.

They began to wrestle, and even though Wayne was much bigger than Trigg, he still had a hard time handling him. Fighting was in Trigg's DNA. All his family could rumble, so it seemed like the genes were passed down from generation to generation. They played that way until they reached their block.

"Yo, bro, I want a rematch 'cause you snuck me and didn't give me a chance to get my guard up."

"That's the whole point. You have to always be ready instead of having to get ready," Tiriq stated. "Them bullies at school isn't gon' give you no time to defend yourself. You always gotta be on point and ready for anything that comes your way. Don't worry, whenever something does pop off, I'll always have your back, lil bro," Tiriq said as they parted ways, heading toward their prospective homes. They were conveniently right across the street from each other.

"Ard, bro, I'll see you tomorrow in Ms. Chambers's class, and I'll bring your fucking sneaks too, nigga," Trigg smirked as he headed in the house.

As soon as he entered the house and set his book bag down, Trigg could hear his mom and dad arguing. It really didn't bother him too much because he was used to it. He headed straight to his room in the basement, which at the moment was part of a moderate two-bedroom house in South Philadelphia. They had been living on 19th and Mountain Street ever since he was two years old. The house was cheap because of the area they were in, and plus it was all they could afford at the time.

Just as he was reaching for the doorknob to the basement, the door swung open, and out came his father looking like he was ready to kill something.

"Dad, where are you going?" Trigg asked as he watched his father walk right past him.

"Stay in the house with your mother, Trigg. I'll be back in a lil while," Tiriq Sr. said as he continued walking toward the front door.

Trigg rushed over to the window, watching his father walk down the street. The look in his eyes made him wonder if he would ever see his father again. Disappointed, he walked away from the window. His mom came out of the basement carrying a laundry basket, and Tiriq could see that she was still crying.

"Mom, what's wrong?" he asked, thinking the worst. She looked up at him with puffy red eyes and just shook her head. Tiriq came over and sat next to her on the couch. "Tell me what's wrong, Ma."

"I can't go to the Salvation Army to get you or your sister's stuff, because your father and I had another big argument. He said he was leaving and never coming back this time," she said as she broke down crying hysterically.

It felt as though reality just kicked in, and his whole life just changed for the worst. Trigg knew that every time his mom and dad argued, his dad would leave, but not once had he ever said that he wasn't coming back. Trigg sat there next to his mother thinking, what positive thing can a fifteen-year-old say to comfort his mother. She was always the strong one in the family, but now was so weak and vulnerable. He placed his arm around her to let her know she wasn't alone and that he was there even if his father wasn't.

"Ma, it's gonna be alright. Dad just needs time to cool off, and he'll be back tonight," he said, not only trying to convince her, but also himself.

She looked up into his eyes, with those light hazel eyes of hers, and just broke down crying again.

"No, son, it's not going to be alright this time. We

have no money, and the job I have is just barely
paying the bills. You and your sister need shoes and
clothes. What are we gonna do if he doesn't come
back home?" she asked with pleading eyes, dying for
an answer he didn't have.

"Don't worry about us, Mom. We'll be fine. Just
take things slowly and it will all work itself out,"
Trigg said, trying to ease some of his mother's pain.
Deep down inside, he felt that this was about to get
even worse than it already was. For some strange
reason that feeling that he felt in the pit of his
stomach was starting to feel like reality. It was all
starting to become clear to him, and he knew what
had to be done. His father wasn't coming back home,
and he was gonna have to step up and be the man of
the house just like his father had been teaching him,
just in case something happened to him. *Real niggas*

do real things! That's what his father always told
him, and now he knew that after tonight, this would
be the breaking point of his young life.

* * *

Trigg's mother stayed up all night drinking and
listening to slow jams, hoping that Trigg's father
came home. As she sat there crying, reminiscing of
the times her and Tiriq Sr. had shared together. Tiriq
was sitting in his room formulating a plan to help his
mother. His mom, Courtney, was half black and half
Puerto Rican. Trigg couldn't figure out why his dad
treated her so badly, because she was the most
beautiful girl Trigg had ever seen.

Courtney had light hazel eyes and long silky hair.
His father was 100 percent African-American, and
was one of the ruthless gangsters left in Philly. They
fell in love with each other in high school, and at the

age of twenty-three and twenty-five, they tied the knot. A few years later Trigg Jr. was born, and then when he turned two, his sister Dajah was born. Trigg's dad gave him the name Trigg because when he was a baby, he would always play with a water gun and never took his finger off the trigger. Now, just like that, they were about to be separated because of something that was still a mystery.

When Trigg woke up the next morning, he found the house really quiet. Usually his lil sister would be running around getting into trouble and his mom would be cooking breakfast.

"Mom, Dajah . . ." he yelled out to them, with no response.

Thinking they were still sleep, he went upstairs to his sister's room first, but she wasn't there. Her bed wasn't made up, which was weird because she always made her bed up in the morning. She would even make his for him sometimes. Next he checked his mother's room, thinking that maybe she had another nightmare, and went to sleep with their mom like she always did. That would explain the unmade bed. He walked in to find her bed was also empty.

"What the fuck is going on? Where the fuck is everyone at?"

Just as he was about to head back out of the room, he noticed a piece of paper sitting on the bed. He picked it up and realized that it was a note to him, from his mom.

To my loving son,

If you are reading this letter then I'm sure you are aware that your sister and I can't live like this, and I want better for her. Your father and I raised you to be strong and know right from wrong. So do the right things, and remember, TRUST NO ONE! Your sister and I love you very much, but now we'll be loving you from a distance. Don't try to come looking for us because you won't find us. It's better this way, because I can't raise you to be a man. Your father left some sneakers for you in the closet. Take care, Tiriq, my handsome son!

Love always,

Your Mother

It was hard for him to read the words in the letter, but he read it again to make sure it wasn't a game. Tears began to run down his face, onto the paper, smearing the ink. When it was all said and done, he got the message loud and clear. Suddenly, anger took over and he started screaming all types of obscene words toward his parents for abandoning him like this. He wondered how he was supposed to take care of himself. He was too young to do anything. How would the bills get paid, and where the hell was he going to get the money for all that? They were the questions that ran through his mind as he sat on his mother's bed. The tears that were flowing freely down his face suddenly stopped, and coldness set in his eyes. From that moment on, he vowed to never shed another tear.

A name popped up in his head, causing him to get an idea, but he would need his friend to be by his side. He had figured out a way to solve all of his problems. He knew that it would take some convincing, and he was up for the challenge.

"I have to go to the streets in order to survive this unfortunate chain of events," he said out loud to no one in particular. "The only way to live is never die, and take over these streets."

Realizing that would be the only way for him to get money because he was too young to work, he made a bold decision and would stick to it. Moe was the neighborhood drug dealer and was very well respected around there. He knew none of the other dealers would give him a chance because they didn't mess around with little kids, but Moe, on the other hand, had a squad of lil niggas. Since he knew him from around the way, he thought it wouldn't be a problem. Moe always wanted Tiriq to be on the team, but Tiriq kept declining. Maybe now he would have a change of heart. Moe was basically his link to his future.

After reading the letter his mother wrote once again, Trigg ripped it up and threw it away. *No more being soft for anyone,* he thought to himself as he looked around his mother's room. It was time for him to become a man, not a boy, so he could do what he had to. *Real niggas do real things* kept replaying in his head as he went into the bathroom to brush his teeth. Those were the words his father said to him for the last fifteen years of his life, and now it was time to put those words to the test.

He came back into his mother's room and lay across the bed staring at the wedding pictures of his mom and dad. That was the time when everything was so peaceful and happy. What went wrong? was the question that he hoped to someday to get the answer to. Before he was able to get to deep in his thoughts, his phone started ringing. He was mad that his thoughts were interrupted, until he saw who was calling him.

"Yo, I need to talk to you about something

ASAP, so come over here as soon as you're dressed," he said to his friend.

"Cool, I'll be over in a few minutes," Wayne replied.

After hanging up the phone, Trigg quickly threw on his school clothes so he would be ready when Wayne came over. He walked over to the closet to see how much stuff his mom took with her, hoping that she left stuff and would have to come back for it. When he opened the closet, his eyes almost popped out of his head. Sitting right on the floor in front of him was a brand-new pair of Jordans. Perspiration began to form all under his arms, and his hands got sweaty. Nervous would be an understatement for what he was feeling right now. He grabbed the box and sat down on the bed, staring at the Jordan logo on the side of the box. Anxiety got the best of him as he opened the box and pulled the pair of sneakers out.

He jumped up in the air hyped as hell, thinking that now he could give Wayne his sneakers back and wouldn't have to hear his mouth again. He was happy his father had purchased his first pair of Jordans. It was fucked up that neither his mom or dad was there to enjoy that moment with him. The ecstatic look on his face was priceless. He looked in the box for the receipt, but only found a letter from his pops.

Yo big guy,

If you're reading this letter, then it's obvious that you got the sneakers I bought for you. I hope you like them, because your little sister picked them out for you. Make sure you thank her. Just so you know, your mother and I weren't seeing eye to eye, so we had to go our separate ways. I thought that would be best for the both of us. It had nothing to do with you or Dajah. Maybe if things work out, we'll be back together. Right now I don't see that happening. Your mother is stubborn, careless, and insecure, and I'm tired of it. I love her more than I love myself, and likewise with you and Dajah, but I'm done, Son. Tiriq, never let anything or anyone come in between you and your sister. That's your blood running through her veins, so protect her with your life. Rock them J's right, and remember that I love you, Son. Most importantly, never forget what I've told you since you were a baby.

Your pops

PS: REAL NIGGAS DO REAL THINGS!

Damn, that letter just fucked his whole train of thought up all over again. He wasn't going to cry again, but he would be frauding if he said his eyes didn't get watery. Trigg knew his dad was a good dude despite walking out on them. He folded the letter up and put it inside his pocket when he heard the door. He knew that it was Wayne that just came in. He grabbed the sneaks that he borrowed and headed downstairs.

"Here's your shit, nigga," Trigg said, passing him the shoes.

"'Bout fucking time," he replied. When he looked down to see what Trigg had on, his eyes got big as hell. "Where you get them from?"

"My pops got them for me."

"Those jawns are hot, bro. I always wanted a pair of those."

Trigg had on some black fitted Levi jeans, laying over his Jordans; a red and white stripe button-down

Polo Ralph Lauren shirt that he had gotten for Christmas last year, and a red Phillies fitted cap to accommodate his outfit. He was ready to show off his new sneaks to the girls in his class.

"That's what I wanted to talk to you about, bro. I have a plan that can get us paid, but you will play a big part in it."

"I'm listening," Wayne said, looking in the refrigerator for something to snack on. "Where's everybody at?"

"Let's go! We'll talk on the way to school," Trigg said, grabbing his bookbag.

Wayne could tell something wasn't right, and whatever it was, he was rocking with his best friend. On their way to school, Trigg told Wayne about everything that happened the day before and what he was planning to do. The idea sounded really appeasing to Wayne, and just like that, they were ready to get money. They decided to go straight to Moe as soon as they got out of school. Everything was ready on their end. They just hoped he would still want to give them a job.

Two

MOE WAS SITTING ON the couch next to some chick he had picked up from the club the night before, when his phone rang. He grabbed it off the nightstand and checked the caller ID to see who it was calling him this early in the morning.

"What's up, Sheed?" he answered.

"Big homie, we need to talk real quick. Are we secure?"

"Hold on for a sec," Moe said, getting up off the bed and walking toward the bathroom. He shut the door and sat on the edge of the sink. "Ard, what's up?"

"The new shipment came in this morning, but they doubled the load. How the fuck are we supposed to move all this shit, and they want to see some results by the end of the week. This shit is crazy, man," Sheed snapped.

Moe and his connect had talked about that yesterday and he told him that he didn't need all that dope right now because of the proceeding beef he had with the Jamaicans in West Philly. They didn't want to give up their blocks, so he planned on taking them. Now since his connect still doubled the shipment, he had to move ASAP to ensure that him and his team could move the product. After he got rid of the Jamaicans, it would be a little easier to move the product.

"Don't worry about it. Grab the team and meet me at the artillery spot. It's time to strap up and go take what we need. Call in our clean-up team too, and tell them to be on standby just in case we need them."

"I'm on it, Moe. See you at the spot," Sheed replied, ending the call.

Moe was pissed because now his hands were tied. He knew better than to play with the cartel's money. He had to do what he had to do now, and it wasn't going to be pretty for his rivals. He told them he would supply them, but they wouldn't listen. Now he was about to take it all and leave them with nothing. He walked out of the bathroom to see the chick lying across the bed with her finger in her pussy, smiling at him.

"I see you started without me, huh?"

"Come join me then," she said, sticking the two fingers she had in her pussy into her mouth.

As much as he wanted to indulge in some more of that good pussy, he had work to do, so that was more important right now. He watched her as she brought herself to another climax as he put his clothes on.

"We can finish up some other time. Right now I have a matter that needs my full attention. Get dressed so I can drop you off," he told her.

She wouldn't take no for an answer though. She hopped of the bed and knelt down in front of him. She glanced up at him as she teasingly licked the tip of his dick, causing him to jerk. Once she was done toying with him, she went to town on his shit. She used one hand to massage his balls, and the other to jack him off while she sucked the tip of his dick.

"Shit, girl," he groaned, grabbing the back of her head and grabbing her hair tight. His lip curled up in pleasure as he watched her wet tongue slurp the sides of his shaft. His veins were protruding through his flesh as she absorbed every inch of his dick down her throat. "Shiiit. Choke on this motherfucker. Daaaamn!" Moe grunted through clenched teeth. She was sucking his dick so good that he forgot all about the meeting he was supposed to be at momentarily.

"Mmmmmm," she moaned, and the vibration from her humming made his balls tingle. If she didn't stop doing what she was doing, he was gonna bust something serious.

Moe continued to enjoy the sight of her stimulating the shit out of his dick. She made sure her mouth was nice and wet. He liked that sloppy toppy. So when she spit on his dick and then slurped it back into her mouth, he groaned loudly. She was a nasty bitch. The echoes of her slurping and gagging bounced off the walls of the bedroom. Tightening the grip on her hair, Moe cursed feeling himself about to cum.

"Shit, here it comes, damn!" Moe cursed, bursting into her warm mouth. "Swallow it. Let me see?" She opened up her mouth, sticking her tongue out so he could make sure she got it all. "Good girl."

Pushing her back lightly, Moe stood to his feet. He stuffed his dick in back into his boxers, then headed over to his closet to grab his clothes.

"What about me?" she asked, watching Moe look through his closet.

"I got you later. I'm gonna pick you up after I finish with this business I have to take care of."

He could tell by the look in her eyes that she wasn't used to being turned down, but there's a first time for everything. Moe dressed in all-black fatigues and his black Polo boots. He grabbed his .40 cal. off the dresser and was ready to go. The chick hurriedly got dressed, and the two of them headed out of the house. After he dropped the girl off and broke her off with a couple of dollars, Moe hopped on the expressway, heading out west. It was game time, and he was ready for war.

* * *

"You motherfuckers know what to do, right?" Moe said to the ten men standing in front of him.

Everyone was dressed up in all black and had on Teflon vests. The room was totally silent as they focused on the task at hand. When Moe was finish going over the game plan, they loaded up in the stolen car and minivan parked outside, and headed over to where Black and his crew were posted up at.

"There they are right there," Sheed stated, pulling out his burner. The other niggas in the minivan with him quickly followed suit. "Air everything out standing there, and don't let none of those clowns come out of this breathing."

Without saying a word, the men jumped out of the van and started laying down everything that was moving. The men never saw it coming. Moe spotted Black sitting in his Mercedes, trying to make a run for it, and rammed straight into him. Moe jumped out of the vehicle and ran up to the driver's side window. Before Black could get himself together from the impact of Moe's vehicle, Moe had the drop on him.

"I asked you to join us, but you didn't want to. Now you have to die," Moe said, aiming his weapon at Black's chest.

"You pussy boy, me not scared to die. Me see you in hell," Black said with a smile on his face.

"Okay, you first," Moe replied, squeezing the trigger.

BOOM! BOOM! BOOM! BOOM!

Black's body convulsed a couple of times before stopping permanently. His head hit the steering wheel, sounding the horn. That told everyone it was time to get the fuck out of there.

"Let's bounce, fellas," Sheed yelled, holding the smoking gun in his hand.

They all jumped back into the vehicles and sped off. Moe sat back in the passenger seat and sparked up the Dutch he brought along. He started thinking to himself that if he had known it would have been that easy, he would have killed Black a long time ago. Little did he know, a storm was brewing, and it was about to be heading in his direction.

* * *

After school, Trigg and Wayne headed down to the bar that Moe owned. It was time to put the next part of the plan in motion. They didn't see his car, which told them he wasn't there yet, so they hung out on the corner waiting.

"Damn, I hope this nigga don't be all day. I'm ready to make some fucking cash, real talk, homie," Wayne said, posted up against the wall.

"Be patient, bro. We don't even know if he's going to put us on yet. If he do give us a chance, we can't blow it. I really need this, Wayne, so we have to make this shit happen."

After what his friend told him, Wayne knew he had to help him. It was fucked up that both of his parents just up and left him out to dry like that. He was going to ask his mom if Trigg could come stay with them, but he knew he wouldn't want to, so whatever his mans needed, he was gonna do.

"I'll be right back. I'm going to the poppi store real quick," Wayne said, walking down the street.

"Bring me a bag of chips and soda."

"Ard, I gotcha, bro."

Trigg stayed at the corner thinking about how he should approach Moe when he got there. He didn't want to just come right out and say he wanted to sell drugs for him, so he decided he would go with a more subtle approach. As he looked around, he could see there was a lot of traffic in the area. People were standing in line just to get the product Moe's people were selling.

"A, boo-boo! Where your daddy at with his fine ass?"

Trigg turned around to see who was talking to him, and immediately his face frowned up at the stench and awful look of this fiend lady named Ms. Sharlene. She looked really bad. She only had her two front teeth left in her mouth from getting them

31

knocked out and was baldheaded. She smelled like she had just played twenty games of ruff outs in the hot-ass sun, and had the nerve to be wearing a little-ass skirt with no panties on. Trigg had to get the fuck away from her before her odor rubbed off on him. She wasn't like that a couple of years ago. She was the baddest bitch walking around Philly, and everybody wanted her. As they say, once these streets get ahold of you, they never let go.

"What's up, Ms. Sharlene. My pops is not home right now, so maybe you should try looking for him some other time," he said, staying as far away from her stinking ass as possible.

"Look at you, looking all fresh and shit. What you around this area for? I know you getting money, so let a bitch get a sample of what you're selling," she said, trying to get closer to him. Trigg kept his distance because he wasn't trying to get smell her anymore. As she talked, spit came out of her mouth. Trigg thought to himself that if any of that shit got on his new sneaks, he was gonna snap the fuck out.

"I don't know what you're talking about. I'm waiting for my friend right now."

"I get my check next week, and I'll pay you then. I know you got something you can let me hold right now," she replied, ignoring what he just told her. "I'll suck your little dick right now if you got five dollars, and you can have some of this pussy if you have ten." She lifted up her skirt, exposing her hairy pussy. Trigg was about to walk away, when Wayne came walking up.

"Get your nut ass out of here before I kick you in it."

"Little boy, you need to watch your mouth. You

lucky I don't go get my son to whip your ass up and down these streets," she shot back.

"Do what you gotta do, bitch. Just get the fuck away from us."

"Come on, Wayne, we have more important things to do than arguing with this lady. I think that's his car coming right there," Trigg said as they saw Moe's car pulling up in front of the bar. They both started walking in that direction.

"A, boo-boo, I'll see you around again! You'll need me one day, looking just like your daddy wit your fine ass. Mmmmm!" she screamed, but they just kept walking without even responding.

They walked up to the bar, and the bouncer that was standing outside had his head down, so they walked right past him and into the bar. That place would surely get shut down if the cops came in and saw two minors inside. As they walked past the threshold, they could see that it was already lit up in there. Dancers were in the back onstage dancing, and it was a crowd of niggas around them. Trigg didn't even know that there was a strip club inside also. This was a surprise to the both of them.

"Look at those bitches, bro," Wayne said excitedly.

"Come on, we have to find Moe before one of these people see that we don't belong in this joint."

They walked past the waitresses that only had thongs on, and headed toward the back of the building, where niggas were playing pool and gambling. Wayne's eyes were glued on the two women on stage molesting each other. Trigg couldn't help but stare also, because they were going ham. He scanned around the bar until he spotted Moe talking to another man that was dressed in a suit. He headed in that direction hoping that everything went his way, or he was assed out.

"We shouldn't have any more problems with those Jamaican pieces of shit. Now we have their territory along with our other spots," Moe told his business partner.

"I'm glad to hear that because we need to move this work, and fast. You're gonna have to hire some more workers to cover all the new areas now."

"I'm gonna take care of that today. I'll meet you at the spot in about an hour so we can go over where everything is going."

"Okay!" the man said, shaking Moe's hand then walking away.

Moe sat there for a few more minutes drinking and watching everything going on in his club, when his eyes stopped on the two young bulls walking in his direction. He wondered how the hell two underage kids were able to enter his establishment. Before they were able to get within ten feet of Moe, some big strong nigga stepped in front of them.

"What the fuck you two lil niggas doing in here? Y'all need to get up out of here before something bad happens. Let's go," he said, grabbing both of their arms.

"We just need to speak with Moe for a minute," Wayne said, yanking his arm away from the bouncer.

"Moe," Trigg yelled out over the loud music. "We need to holla at you for a minute please." The bouncer still had his hand on Trigg was trying to pull him away.

Trigg didn't like the fact that the big bouncer put his hands on him, and without even thinking, a right jab caught the bouncer right in the nose.

"Awww, I'ma kill you little motherfuckers," he screamed, and came charging at them like a raging bull.

Little did he know Trigg's father had taught him well. Trigg sidestepped him, then kicked him in the back of his knees, bringing him down to their size. Next Trigg hit him with a combination that any father would have been proud of, knocking the big man out. Before they had a chance to do anything else, four men had cannons out, aimed at their heads. Not wanting to die, neither one of them moved. They just stood there looking around hoping someone would come to their rescue.

"Whoa, chill out, not in this place. There are too many witnesses up in here. Sonny should have been dipping and dodging, but he got knocked the fuck out by some lil nigga," Chubb, Moe's right-hand man said. He looked over at Moe to see what he wanted to do with these two young bulls.

Moe was really impressed by these two lil niggas' aggressiveness and signaled for his workers to lower their guns and let them through. They walked over to where Moe was seated and stood in front of him.

"First off, I don't know how the hell you two got up in this motherfucker, but it better be for a good motherfucking reason," he stated, taking another sip of his liquor before setting the glass on the table. "Who taught you how to fight like that?"

"My dad," Trigg said proudly.

Moe stared at him for a long hard minute, trying to recognize where he knew this kid from. Then it hit him.

"Your father is Tiriq right?" Trigg nodded his head yes. "Damn, you're Tiriq Jr. Me and your father used to go to the same school. That nigga would fuck up anybody that crossed him. Now I see where you got those moves from. So what brings y'all here?"

"I was coming to ask you some serious questions about a situation I'm having, but that dickhead started talking crazy to me and my friend. I'm sorry for the way I reacted, but my pops always told me, never let anyone put their hands on you."

"You almost got yourself killed too, if it wasn't for me. See where moving without thinking can lead you?" Moe stated, dropping a little knowledge on the both of them.

The whole time everything was jumping off, Wayne was standing in the background watching. He was already hip to how his friend got down, so he didn't even have to react. Trigg was trained for combat. That's why no one in school fucked with them.

"I just needed to holla at you real quick," Trigg said, hoping Moe would agree.

"Hold up for a second," Moe said, turning toward his men. "Help that nigga up and take him in the back to get his self together. The rest of you get back to work while I talk to these two young lions." Wayne and Trigg looked at each other with a smile on their face, already knowing what the next one was thinking. "Follow me, fellas. That was a pretty right hand you got there, young buck."

"Thank you!"

"That wasn't a compliment. I was just stating facts. Now what did you want to talk about that it nearly cost you your life?"

"Mr. Moe, I, or rather we, need your help because a situation came up that needs immediate attention. I know you and my father was cool and you told him that if he ever needed anything, just ask."

"Oh, no doubt. What do big Riq need?" Moe asked, pulling out a wad of cash.

"He doesn't need anything. We do."

"What kind of things you—wait, don't answer that, because I think I already know. I'll tell you what, if you can beat her," Moe said, pointing to some chick, "in a game of pool, then we can sit down and really talk, but if you lose, y'all leave my club and never come back. Deal?" Moe said, propositioning them.

Trigg had to think about it for a minute. He had never played pool before so he thought Moe was being unfair. He was no quitter though, so he agreed by shaking hands with the devil.

"Deal!"

Moe signaled for the chick to come over. When they looked at the girl, she was the same one that was just onstage getting at the money. He knew it was gonna be one of the hardest missions he was yet to face.

"Yes, daddy?" the chick said, sashaying over to them, with only a thong on. It was hard for Trigg and Wayne to keep their eyes off the redheaded beauty. She was bad as shit, standing at five foot six, with a phat ass, and her body was tatted up.

"Do me a favor, love: play this lil nigga in a game of pool, and don't take it easy on him either," he said as she bent over and kissed him on the cheek.

"Y'all some cuties. I ain't never seen you around here before. What's up with these lil dudes?" she asked.

"Don't even worry about it right now. Just handle your business." Moe stated frankly.

They followed the stripper over to the pool table. The whole time neither one of them took their eyes off of her ass. Wayne was stuck in a trance as his blood pressure rose, causing his manhood to rise.

"You look like something got you excited," the stripper said, pointing to the bulge growing in his jeans. Her smile was fucking these kids' heads up. To add more tension between them, she grabbed Trigg's dick then whispered in his ear. "If you win, I might give you a bonus prize, so don't get too distracted." Before moving away, she licked his ear for inspiration.

"Come on, let's get this game poppin'." Wayne said, ready to get the fuck out of there.

"Ard, grab a stick and let's play," she said, setting up the balls on the table. Once she was done, she looked over to Trigg. "You break, baby."

"You break. I don't know how to do that."

"Watch and learn," she said before picking up her stick.

When she bent over the table to break the balls, Wayne stared at her pussy lips. She hit the balls, knocking three of them into the hole. Then she moved around and hit another and another. When she finally missed a shot, she looked over to Trigg.

"Your turn, cutie," she replied with a smile.

Trigg stepped up to take a shot, and missed. The ball flew off the table and landed on the floor. Wayne and Moe laughed at him as they watched Trigg make a complete ass of himself from a distance.

"Looks like we have a rookie, huh, daddy?"

"Yeah, I tried to tell him you was the best in the city, but he insisted on playing you," Moe lied.

Trigg shot him a look as if to say, "Nigga, you a lying fraud." Moe picked up on the stare and winked his eye at him, letting him know he was only talking shit.

"Is that right? Well I guess I have to show him that I'm not just a pretty face, and watch him leave here with a bitter taste in his mouth. She threw a leg on the table and bent over giving them a clear view of her ass and pussy lips. "You like what you see?"

She hit every shot after that, and won the game. Wayne was in total shock at the way she just handled his man on that table.

"Well, my friend, seems like she just sealed the deal. Tell your father I said hi when you see him, and I'll see you around," Moe said, getting up to shake

Trigg's hand.

"You tried, cutie, maybe next time. I hope you're not that fast in bed," she said, giving his dick a squeeze then walking away. Moe smacked her on the ass as she passed by him.

"Good job, sexy."

"No problem, daddy. You know I can't be fucked with. I'm the best thing around here when it comes to that pool shit."

"Ard, lil nigga, you had your fun, seen your first shot of real pussy, now it's time to go. Too bad you lost, because I think she would of probably let you hit, even though I know you wouldn't know what to do with that pussy. This the first time in a while that I seen her all up in some nigga's face. I think she likes you, but you will never get to taste that pussy. She needs a man with some money, lil man, and you don't have any. Well, don't take it personal, but a deal is a deal, and you and your friend have to get up out of here. Don't try that bullshit that you did earlier, because next time I may not be able to save you."

"But, Moe, I need your help," Trigg said with pleading eyes. "Some shit came up with me, and I really need to make some moves."

"Then you should have won. Now go home, lil Riq, and tell your parents I said happy holidays," he replied, pulling a fifty-dollar bill from his pocket and handing it to Trigg.

Trigg couldn't even say anything else but "thank you." As him and Wayne headed toward the door, the stripper that beat him in pool was sitting at the bar drinking.

"Hey cutie, I'll see you next time, and maybe you'll win and I can keep my word and give you what

I owe you," she said, then blew him a kiss.

"You're gonna have that kid going home with blue balls if you don't stop that bullshit," Moe said to the stripper as she walked away switching.

"I'm not doing anything," she said, smiling.

Trigg left out of there blushing, hoping and praying she'd keep her word when he was able to beat her. He vowed that he wouldn't let anyone else beat him at anything. He had gained more knowledge than he came in with, and soon he was going to use it on everybody to get what he wanted.

Three

TRIGG WOKE UP THE next morning to the sound of his alarm clock, and quickly realized that he was still home alone. He had been sleeping in his parents' bed the last few nights, hoping that one of them would wake him up and kick him out. He hopped up and got in the shower to get ready for school. He was so tired from the chain of events that went down last night that he started not to go.

After getting dressed, he fixed himself a bowl of Fruity Pebbles, then sat at the table watching ESPN. He watched the highlights from the Dallas/Giants game that he fell asleep on last night, until he was finished eating. Dallas had beat up on his team 19–3. Around 7:30, Trigg walked out of the house and ran right into Ms. Sharlene again.

"Good morning, boo-boo. Is your daddy in the house?" she asked Trigg.

He couldn't even answer because his stomach instantly started doing summersaults as she blew her stinking breath into his face. His breakfast was seconds away from coming back up.

"Naw, he not here. He went to work already, and my mom's not here either, sorry," Trigg said as he tried hard to hold his breath until he could get away from her.

She continued walking down the street looking for someone that would help support her habit. Making sure he locked the door behind him, he headed over to Wayne's house to see if he was ready. Usually he would come get him, but today Trigg had something different in mind.

"Hey, boo-boo, come see me later. I have something for you," Ms. Sharlene yelled out to him as she started walking back down toward him.

Trying to hurry up and get away, he knocked, then walked right into Wayne's crib. He knew his mom wouldn't mind because he had done it plenty of times before. He went straight upstairs to Wayne's room to see if he was ready. He walked in on him trying to dance in the mirror.

"Damn. nigga, is this the reason why you weren't at my crib?" Trigg said. laughing at his friend.

"Naw, I'm just practicing my moves for Friday. You are still going with me, right?" Wayne asked Trigg as he sat on the bed and threw on his sneakers.

"Hell yeah I'm going. I wouldn't miss that shit for the world. I'm going to clown your ass as soon as you lose," Trigg replied.

"What's up with that situation though?" Wayne asked on some serious shit.

"I'll figure something out today. I just have to think of another game plan to come at him, or try to find someone else that can connect me with him."

"Come on before we're late; then I'll have to hear my mom's mouth, and you know how she is," Wayne said, heading downstairs with Trigg on his heels.

As they walked down the street, Trigg's mind was going a hundred miles an hour as he tried to figure out how he was going to get close to Moe again. He knew if he could just get put on, all of his worries would be placed in the back of his mind. What really kept playing in his little head was what that dancer did. She had him turned out, and all she did was grab his lil mans. Trigg was anticipating his next encounter with her sexy ass. He wondered what her name was because Moe never said it. He couldn't wait to get his money up, because she was going to be the first person he bagged. He was so caught up in his thoughts that he didn't hear Wayne talking to him, until they were a block away from their school.

"Damn, motherfucker, I was talking to you and you was lost in la la land somewhere. Is everything alright, bro?"

"Yeah, I'm straight, bro. I was just thinking about that bitch from last night," Trigg said as they walked into the building, waiting to go through the metal detector.

"Man, I would love to lose my virginity to her. She probably have my ass chasing her all over Philly," Wayne said. Both of them burst out laughing.

Once they went through the metal detector, they

dapped each other up, then headed toward their advisory classes. Trigg made his mind up that after school he was going to pay Moe another visit. This time he was going to get his point across, and not be told to keep it moving.

* * *

"Good morning, class. Would everyone please open their science books to page 345. Today we will be going over our solar system and the universe. I'm assuming everyone studied for the test you will be having today," Ms. Hannah stated as everyone began opening their books up. "After the test, we will all head over to the gym for your physical education class."

Trigg, along with everyone else, slouched back in their seats while Ms. Hannah was writing on the board. She was an older woman with streaks of gray hair in her brown dreadlocks. Her skin was a smooth mahogany color, and she was physically fit for her age. If you didn't know her age, you would swear that she was no older than thirty-five.

"Yo, what you doing after school?" James whispered to Trigg, who was pretending like he was studying for his test. "My mom said that y'all could come over and hang out."

"James, you're gonna be the first to volunteer to read since you have so much to talk about," Ms. Hannah said, catching him trying to whisper to Trigg. She smiled at them, showing off her pearly white teeth.

"Um, sure thing, Ms. Hannah. I don't mind reading first," James responded, blushing from embarrassment.

"Good, we'll begin as soon as I finish writing this

stuff on the board. Tiriq, you better not be talking behind my back, or you will be following right behind your classmate."

While the teacher turned back toward the board to finish writing, Trigg and James secretly continued to hold their conversation until their teacher was ready to begin. James begged him until he finally gave in, and gave him two thumbs-up.

After the teacher finished what she was doing, she turned to James and told him to begin reading. Even though he wasn't a good reader, he tried his best, and when he was done, Trigg took over and finished. While they took a short break, Trigg stared out the window, and when he was about to turn around to go back to his seat, something made him do a double take. He hurried back over to the window, but she was gone. He thought he had seen his mother standing by a tree. He thought he was hallucinating, or was it really her standing there as if she was checking up on him?

Thinking that maybe he was seeing things, Trigg walked back over to his seat and opened his textbook back up to take some final notes before the test. It didn't really matter because he always cheated off the girl next to him, who was one of the smartest people in the class. He would make sure that he got at least a few answers wrong on purpose so the teacher didn't get suspicious. The girl knew what he was doing, but didn't care because she had a little schoolgirl crush on him anyway.

Once class was over, Trigg went to his locker to put his books away. When he opened the door, there was a note with hearts all over it, hanging halfway out. Confused, he looked around to see if someone was watching him, but everyone seemed to be occupied in their own lil world. There was one girl that was staring in his direction, but when he noticed her, she turned away and headed back down the hallway. Trigg went into the bathroom and locked himself into one of the stalls so he could read the letter. He was hoping that after he read it, he would have an idea of who wrote it.

He opened it up and began reading it:

Hey my love,

When you walked into the class, my heart dropped the moment I laid eyes on you. I am so in love with you. I had this crush since the second grade, but you never paid me no mind. Why . . . ? Am I ugly or something to you? Is it because I'm not skinny like these other bitches? Let me know and I will do what I need to do. I look better than half the girls in this school, and I dress better. So what seems to be the problem with me? Do you already have a girlfriend, Trigg? When you get a chance, write me back. I'm sure you know who this is now.

Taya

PS: Do you like me, yes or no? (circle one)

Trigg came out of the bathroom, looking around to see if anybody was watching him, because he was blushing hard as fuck. He was embarrassed that someone would see the soft side of him. When he walked into his next class, him and Taya made eye contact instantly. She smiled and Trigg smiled back. Upon further inspection of her, he realized just how pretty she really was. The only problem he had was that she was a little on the chunky side.

"Okay, class, line up so we can go over to the gym," Ms. Hannah said after gathering her purse and cell phone.

Trigg wasn't really feeling the whole gym thing because he was trying to get out of there so he could catch up to Moe again. He lined up next to James, then Taya came over and stood next to him. He got nervous and scared. For a second, he thought she was going to eat him the way she was staring. Trigg took a step to his left away from her, and James smiled.

"I'm not gonna eat you," Taya said as if she was reading his mind. "Unless you want me to."

She licked her lips, smiled, then walked away to kick it with her friends. As soon as she wasn't in ear's reach, James started his bullshit.

"Okay, bro, I see you. She's a bit on the chunky side, but do your thing, playa," James said, laughing at his friend. "You know who her brother is, right?"

"No, should I care?" Trigg asked, getting irritated with his friend.

"No, you don't have to care that her brother is that nigga Moe," James said as they sat down on the bleachers watching everyone else work out.

The mention of Moe's name quickly got Trigg's attention. He looked at James as if he was wrong or something. He stared, momentarily wondering if he just heard wrong or not.

"Did you just say that she is related to Moe?"

"That's his little sister, Trigg. How the fuck you didn't know that? He's just never around her because of all the enemies he accumulated from the drug business. I guess I can see why you didn't know this."

"How the hell do you know then?" Trigg asked

curiously.

"Because unlike you, I talk to these bitches," James smirked. "You're too busy running around with Wayne doing nothing while I'm out here trying to fuck all these hot chicks."

"Whatever, man, I think I just figured out a way to get Moe to holla at me. I need you to do something for me, and once I get put on, you will also."

"What do you need me to do?"

Four

TAYA AND HER FRIENDS were walking home from school laughing and talking about what had transpired in class earlier. All of them had lil crushes on Trigg, but were too scared to approach him. Taya was the one with the biggest crush, so she stepped up to the plate and sent him a love letter. Once he saw the letter and smiled at her, she knew that one day he would be hers. She told herself she would shed all those extra pounds just to be with him. When they reached the corner of her block, everyone went their separate ways.

As Taya was walking toward her house, out of nowhere some dude dressed in dirty clothes tried to snatch her purse. She tried to hold onto it, but he was too strong for her.

"Somebody help me," Taya screamed.

"Yo, get the fuck away from her," someone yelled.

The man turned around and saw two young bulls running toward him. He quickly dropped the purse and ran in the opposite direction. When Taya looked up, Trigg and Wayne were rushing in her direction. She was still a bit hysterical about what had just happened and was shaking profusely.

"Are you okay?" Trigg asked, picking up her purse.

"I think so," she replied as Trigg gave her the purse. "Thank you for helping me."

"Come on, we'll walk you home."

"I only live right there," Taya said, pointing to the red brick house sitting in the middle of the block.

"That's cool! We're just gonna make sure nobody else tries to do anything stupid to you before you get there," Trigg replied.

"Thanks!" was all she could say. She was more than grateful that it was Trigg that saved her from getting mugged. But whoever that dirty nigga was, was gonna get his once she told her brother what happened.

"See you in school tomorrow," Trigg said once she walked up on her porch to go in the house.

"Okay," she replied, watching him and Wayne walk down the street.

Her pussy was soaked just thinking about what it would be like to have sex with Trigg. She waited until they turned the corner, before going in the house. As soon as she closed the door, Moe was coming out of the kitchen with a turkey and cheese sandwich and a big bag of chips. He only came over to check up on his mom and sister once a week. Taya dropped her book bag and purse to the floor and rushed over into his arms.

"Damn, why you so happy to see me? I was just over here a few days ago," he said, taking a step back from her. He was about to go sit down, until he saw the tears in her eyes. "What's wrong?"

"Someone tried to mug me."

"When?" Moe said, setting his food down on the coffee table. He grabbed his gun from under the pillow and cocked it.

"Just a few minutes ago, but Tiriq and Wayne came before he could get away, then walked me home."

"What this motherfucker look like so I can have my people look out for him?"

"He looked like a bum," Taya replied.

Moe wrapped his arms around her and held her. She was his only sister, and he'd be damned if he would let anything happen to her. At first he thought it was one of his competitors trying to send a message, until she said it was a bum. His mind was still thinking that maybe it was one of them trying to disguise themselves. He was going to put his ears to the streets just in case it was something else going on that he would need to address.

"If anybody ever tries that shit again, you better use that Taser I gave you," Moe said, releasing his grip and sitting down on the couch. "Where is it at anyway?"

"Upstairs in my room," she said hesitantly, knowing that he was about to chew her head off for not carrying it with her. To her surprise, he didn't. He just reached into his pocket and pulled out a wad of cash and passed it to her.

"Put that up with the rest of my stuff. If you or Mommy need anything, just take it from that, okay?" Taya nodded her head in agreement. "If you see that motherfucker again, give me a call ASAP, and make sure you keep that Taser or the mace on you at all times when you're out in those streets."

"Okay, Moe, I will," she replied, kissing him on the cheek.

Moe grabbed the rest of his sandwich and headed for the door. He turned around just as he opened the door and told his sister that he loved her, just like he always did. Taya knew the routine and waited to hear those famous words. She smiled, and as soon as he closed the door, she ran upstairs to put the cash away in the safe that he had built in her room. The only two people that knew it was there, or the combination to it, were her and Moe.

* * *

"That was lit how you grabbed her bag and tried to run with all those dirty-ass clothes on," Trigg stated as they stood by the bodega conversing.

"It wouldn't have been so lit if she knew it was you, and told her brother. Your ass would have been lying in the morgue somewhere waiting for your parents to come identify the body," Wayne smirked.

He didn't think it was a good idea to fuck around with Moe like that because they could all end up dead if he ever found out who was behind the mugging. They were just trying to scare her and hoped she would tell her brother that they were the ones who saved her.

"That's why I wore this," James replied, holding up the mask he used. "She didn't see my face at all. Trigg, just don't forget about me if he puts you on, bro."

"Nigga, I said I got you, now just keep your mouth closed. We'll see you in school tomorrow, bro." They all dapped fists with each other. Then Trigg and Wayne headed in the direction of their home, while James headed back toward the school to get ready for football practice.

"I think we should go hang out around the bar. Hopefully we can see that chick doing her thing again. That bitch was bad, real talk," Wayne said, rubbing his hands together like it was cold outside.

"That's cool, but I need to run to the crib real quick and grab something," Trigg said as they turned on their block. Trigg ran in the house, then returned a couple of minutes later dressed differently. He had on a pair of gray Nike sweatpants, with a black hoodie. He kept his Js on so he could continue showing them off. "You're not gonna change out of your school clothes?"

Wayne looked at him like he was crazy, then faked like he was putting up his middle finger, and punched Trigg in the arm. The two friends played like they were fighting all the down the street. Once they were on Moe's block, they acted like they weren't paying any attention to the club, nor the people that were coming in and out.

"How long are we gonna sit out here and wait?" Wayne asked.

"You're the one that wanted to come, and now

you're asking how long we gonna be here? I'm going to stay until I see him pull up, then ask him again."

"Okay, you know I'm with you, bro. It's whatever with me."

"Let's grab some chips and a soda while we're sitting here waiting," Trigg said, walking into the Bodega.

Wayne followed behind his friend and stood by the door. He wanted to keep an eye out for when Moe pulled up. They were trying to catch him before he went in the club, because they knew they wouldn't be able to get in there. After Trigg grabbed the stuff, they went back outside and posted up on the corner like they owned it.

The drug traffic out there was lit. Fiends were coming from every angle, with their money in hand looking for that good shit. As the traffic got thicker, so did the workers. A couple more young bulls came out of the club to make sure their team was okay.

Trigg could see the many ratchets hanging from their jackets. They watched all the fiends copping from the corner boys and were hoping that it would soon be them serving all those thirsty addicts.

Five

ASHLEY HAD BEEN STANDING outside her job for over an hour. She had called Moe's phone repeatedly, to no avail. Co-workers walked by giving her the same sympathetic look they gave her every day. Some offered rides, while others asked if she was alright, but she held her head high and declined any assistance. Finally her phone rang and she picked it up.

"Damn, what the fuck you been blowing my phone up for?" Moe asked.

"You know why I'm calling . . . I've been off work for an hour, and once again no ride. Why else would I be blowing up your phone?" she answered.

"I got caught up handling business and then had to rush and pick something up," Moe retorted.

Ashley started to argue with him, but didn't

because she needed some money from him later when she went out with her friends.

"Are you on your way to pick me up now, or do I have to figure out another way home?" she asked sarcastically.

"I'm still out, but your ride should be pulling up any minute now."

Just as Moe was finishing that statement, a brand-new Jay-Z-blue Lincoln Navigator turned the corner and pulled up right in front of Ashley. The driver jumped out, then hopped in the car that was following him, and pulled off leaving the Navigator running. She stood there looking at the truck, thinking that the two guys stole somebody's shit and left it there.

"Ash, did your ride get there yet?"

"No, some dude just jumped out of a Navi and got into some other car and pulled off," Ashley replied, still staring at the Navi. That was her favorite color, and it was also the kind of vehicle she wanted. "When will it be here, babe? I'm ready to go home and get in the shower."

"It's already there," Moe stated.

Ashley looked around, and when she didn't see no other vehicle approaching, she looked at the Lincoln again. That's when it hit her. A big-ass smile came over her face as she started screaming into the phone, causing the people walking past to look at her.

"Thank you, thank you, thank you, baby," Ashley said, hopping in the driver's seat. "When you get home, I have a special surprise for you. Just make sure you're there before six."

Ashley wanted to show her appreciation to her man, then she definitely was going to go out and show off her new car anyway. Besides, Friday was her birthday, and since she had off, she was going to turn the fuck up.

"I'll see you soon then, love you!"

"Love you too!"

She pulled up at the front entrance to her job, where she knew all her haters would be waiting for her, and pretended she had left something in her locker. Just as she expected, all eyes were on her when she stepped out of the Navigator. She nonchalantly walked into the building knowing they were all gawking over her vehicle. Her pussy got wet just from the thought. She couldn't wait to release all the excitement she was feeling on her man.

When Ashley came back out from her locker, two of her co-workers were waiting for her. They walked up to her, but she didn't give them a chance to speak.

"Like my birthday present from my man?" she bragged.

"That shit is hot, Ash. Do that, girl," the one that used to feel sorry for her said.

Ashley could tell she wanted to ask her to take them for a spin, but she had other things to handle.

"I'll see y'all on Monday. Have a good weekend." Ash jumped back in the Navigator and pulled out in traffic playing Young M.A's "OOOUUU" with everyone's eyes all on her. Those past two months of feeling embarrassed, waiting for Moe to pick her up, was just all forgiven. She was about to break out her new Victoria's Secret lingerie for tonight. It was on.

* * *

Moe came in that night after twelve. He knew he was wrong for staying out so late, and wanted to try and make it up to Ashley. He walked into the bedroom, and she was lying there peacefully under the covers. He reached over and slowly slid the covers back to expose her pale, beautiful body. Ashley was a heavy sleeper, but he knew just how to wake her up. Once she was free from the covers, he hovered over her, careful not to put all of his weight on her. He leaned down and wrapped his lips around her nipple, then sucked it until it hardened in his mouth. Moe heard her moan, but she didn't stir or open her eyes, so he sucked a little harder and then switched to her other nipple. She started to squirm, so he made a trail of kisses from between her titties down to her belly button, where he stopped and took a dip in.

"Ummmm," she moaned. That was a sensitive spot and Moe knew it. He always picked at her because she always had the weirdest spots.

Moe kissed his way down to her thighs and took his hands and spread her legs slightly. He then encircled her clit with his tongue and lightly sucked.

"Sssss shit."

Moe peeked up, and she was leaning up watching him. That was his cue to kick it up a notch. He licked and sucked until he heard her say every curse word you could think of in one sentence, and shortly after, her legs were trembling and she was filling up his mouth with her sweet nectar.

"Oh my God, baby, shit," she panted, trying to get herself together.

"I ain't done." He looked up and smirked at her, and she threw herself back on the bed. Moe wiped his mouth with the back of his hand and climbed in between her legs. "I want you to know that I love you no matter what happens. You mean the world to me, and I will do anything to make you happy."

"Baby, is everything okay? You act like this is the last time you're gonna be in this pussy," Ashley moaned.

"Yeah, ma, I just wanted you to know that."

Moe placed his dick at her opening, and she was soaked and anxiously awaiting his penetration. He took a deep breath, then slid in nice and slow. Sex with Ashley was always amazing, which was why he never had to worry about it being boring in the sack. He shook that thought off immediately, and began to move slowly in and out of her wet tunnel. He moved his hips in a circular motion, wanting to make sure he hit every spot she had. He needed her to feel him at this moment. Not that sex fixes things, but he just wanted to show her what she meant to him and what he was feeling at that moment.

"You make me feel so good, baby," she moaned, with her nails piercing his back. He bit his bottom lip to endure the pain. Moe had already told her about those pointy-ass nails.

"That's my fucking job." He grabbed her waist and lifted her up off the bed a little so he could get better access. She spread her legs a little more, and Moe grinded into her pussy. All you could hear were her screams and the sound of his dick working the shit out of her soaking wet pussy. "Fuck, Ashley, it's so good."

"Handle your pussy, daddy," she taunted. He pulled out and slapped her on the leg. She already knew what it was. She rolled over and tooted that ass up just right, arching her back just the way he liked it. Moe eased back into her pussy, and had to stop for a second as she drenched his dick.

He grabbed her ass cheeks and spread them, watching as he slid in and out of her. The way his dick shined with her juices did something to him, and caused him to speed up. He worked her ass for a good thirty minutes until he was pulling out and cumming all over her back.

"Why did you do that?" Ashley asked, lying on her stomach because her back was covered with nut.

"Do what?" Moe said out of breath. That session took a lot out of him, and if he didn't have shit to do, he would take his ass to sleep. He needed to go count that money and make sure it was right for when he met up with his connect in the morning.

"Cum on my back, nigga," she asked, and he knew where this conversation was about to go.

Ashley wanted to try for another baby, and he wasn't trying to have any more at this time. He had his own reasons for not wanting any kids right now, but kept them to himself. She had just had a miscarriage last year, and it almost killed her. Now she wanted to take that risk once again. Moe felt like they needed more time, but Ash wasn't trying to hear that shit.

"Ash, I don't want to do this right now."

"Do what, talk? What's new?" she replied sarcastically.

"What the fuck's that supposed to mean?"

"When shit gets tough and ain't what you want to hear, you run or shut down. That's what it means. You know what I want, Moe."

"I told you before that ain't gonna happen right now, so drop this conversation. I'm going to take a shower and get ready for tomorrow morning."

Moe quickly left the room before Ashley had a

chance to say anything else. He thought he was going to come home and everything would be alright, but it wasn't. The shower was running and the bathroom was steamy. He could hear Ashley sobbing silently in the other room. He hated when she cried, and went back in the room to comfort her. They were just getting over one miscarriage, and he would hate for her to suffer another one. That would destroy both of them, and that was something he didn't want to happen.

"Ash, I don't want to do this. I'm only trying to protect you."

"I don't need you to protect me. I need you to love me enough to want to build with me."

"You know I want that, more than anything in this world. I just don't want you to go through another miscarriage. I told you that time and time again."

"Why do you keep saying you don't want *me* to

go through it, like I'm in this by myself?"

"You know I ain't even saying it like that. I'm just saying that I'm not the one that has to go through the whole shit. I think we need to just fall back and wait awhile."

Moe was trying to tell her exactly how he felt. He didn't think it was a good time to try because he didn't know if she would survive another disappointment like she had before. This might fuck her up mentally, emotionally, and physically, but she wasn't trying to see it that way. He needed to watch his words carefully because this was what caused the last big fight they had.

"That's your favorite line: we should wait." She jerked her arm away from his. "I don't want to wait. I found this good doctor, and he said we have a good chance to keep the baby now. He started me on some hormone therapy already."

"And when were you going to tell me?"

"I'm telling you now!" she shot back.

"Okay, okay." Moe sighed heavily. "If that's what you want, that's what we'll do. We can start right now if it will make you happy. Just don't get your hopes up." As soon as the words left his mouth, he regretted them.

Ashley stormed out of the room and slammed the door behind her. Moe just sat there trying to figure out a way to make her happy again. He already bought her the truck she wanted, and knew that the only other thing she wanted in the whole world was another child. He was gonna make sure his wife was happy by any means necessary.

Six

"YO, SHIT GETTING HOT and we gone have to switch that shit up, and quick," Chubb said, getting straight to the point, not wanting to beat around the bush. Shit was getting hot, and he wasn't trying to be caught up in no bullshit. He wasn't no bitch, but he wasn't trying to go to war with law enforcement either.

"Whoa, whoa, just calm down. Let's talk," Moe said, giving him a look before turning around and heading back toward his office. "Shut the door behind you, and have a seat so we can talk about this."

Chubb shut the door and took a seat opposite Moe's desk. Once he was seated, he started breaking down what had happened last night at the club.

"Look, Moe, the police ran up in the club talking about they were looking for drugs and shit. What the fuck, man? I don't even know how they knew we were pushing shit from there."

"It's simple. They either have an informant or they were watching motherfuckers that don't even belong in there running in and out. How many people did they get?" Moe asked.

"They locked up a couple of our young niggas that were hanging in the back of the building, but that was it."

"Go get them out and start doing your fucking job so nothing like this ever happens again," Moe snapped.

"First off, I was doing my fucking job, and who the fuck is you talking to like that? I'm not those pussies you have working out there. I'll lay your ass out where you sit, nigga. We are partners in this shit. I don't work for you, so stop acting like it," Chubb threatened. "What we need to do is keep the shit that we have going on on the side, out of there."

"Hell no, we're not letting no fucking pigs stop

our motherfucking money, and just so you know, this is my business. You may have helped me get to where I am, but I'm still the head motherfucking honcho around here."

"Nigga, fuck you. I don't have to listen to this shit you're talking. I have a lot of shit going on right now and don't have time for this," Chubb said, getting up to leave. As he was walking away, he heard a gun cock. He stopped in his tracks and turned around, looking at Moe. "It's like that now?"

"If that's how you make it." Moe shrugged his shoulders.

"You know the rules to the game: don't pull it if you're not going to use it."

"I hope I never have to," Moe said, hoping he got his point across.

Chubb didn't bother responding. He didn't know what he had gotten himself into, but one thing he did know was that he was going to have to take care of Moe before he found out that everything that happened was because of him.

* * *

Trigg and Wayne were walking down the street toward the Bodega when Moe pulled up next to them and rolled the window down.

"Yo, lil nigga, let me holla at you for a minute," he said.

Trigg and Wayne walked over to the car to see what he wanted. He was counting money from a bankroll he had removed from the glove compartment. He passed it to Trigg.

"That's for protecting my little sister the other day. I bet you didn't even know she was my sister, did you?" Trigg shook his head no. "Anyway, she told me that y'all are in the same class and that you treat her with the utmost respect. For that, you have my respect, and I also want to extend my generosity by offering both of you a job. If you can handle the little things that I'll have you doing, then I'll give you more responsibility. Do you still want the job, or what?"

"Hell yeah," they both said in unison.

"Okay, get in so I can show y'all what you will be doing and put you to work," Moe said, unlocking the door.

Both Wayne and Trigg climbed in and closed the door behind them. They rode around for about an hour as Moe filled them in on everything they would be doing. It was a lot to take in, but they didn't mind at all as long as they were getting paid. Moe felt like he could trust them and even showed them where the safe house was. That was something the rest of his workers didn't even know. The only people that knew about the safe house were Moe and Chubb. Now it was four. After driving around for a while, they stopped at TGIF to grab something to eat.

"This is where all the stars come, right?" Trigg asked as they walked inside.

"Most, but they also go to other places down here. Order whatever you want to get. It's on me this time," Moe replied.

"Bet I already know what I want," Wayne said, rubbing his hands together as if he was cold.

They stayed there for over an hour while Moe talked about shit, just kicking it with the two young bulls. The more he talked to Trigg, the more he was beginning to like him. He really had his head on right to be so young. Wayne was wise also to be so young, so he knew he made the right decision by grabbing these two. When Moe dropped them off back on their block, he told them to make sure they were ready to work after school tomorrow. School was a must in Moe's eyes. He didn't want either of them to miss any days. If they did, it better be for a good reason, or they were cut off.

"Yo, I told you this would be our meal ticket. We fucking on now, bro," Trigg stated, smacking Wayne on his back.

"What are you going to buy with the money he gave you? I know what I'm getting," Wayne said.

"I'm going to stack my money, bro. I have something special planned, and trust me, niggas going to be tight about it. I'm about to go in the crib and take a shower, then fall back and catch the game or something."

"Who plays tonight?"

"Dallas and Arizona! I forgot, my Eagles smoked your Giants yesterday. I told you they were going to get their asses whipped," Trigg bragged.

"Fuck you, nigga. That lucky-ass field goal they got. I was fucking pissed about that shit, but it is what it is. Y'all won round one, but we will win round two."

"And my man Carmelo got traded to OKC. I'm going to miss him, but at least he's in a better place now."

"Yeah, that just boosted OKC's chances this year. They're definitely going to be the team to fuck with this year. I can't wait until the season starts. But I'll holla at you tomorrow, bro."

Trigg went in the crib and tried to turn the light on, but it wouldn't come on. He thought it was the breaker and went into the basement to check it. After checking the breaker, he realized that the electric had gotten turned off. He remembered seeing the bills on the table, but didn't pay them any mind.

"Fuck!" he screamed out.

After a couple of minutes, he remembered that one of the fiends down the street knew how to turn the electric on illegally. He went back outside to find him. Trigg was glad that he had some money, but mad at the same time that he was going to have to use some of it for this bullshit. It was either that or go through the night with no lights or television, and that was something he wasn't trying to do. He found white boy Scotty standing on the corner with that dirty stinking fiend Sharlene. As much as he didn't want to see this bitch, he had no choice.

"Scotty, I need to holla at you real quick."

"What's up, young blood?" Scotty asked.

"Can you turn my power back on. I got you," Trigg said.

"I got you, buck. Let me grab my tools. I'll be right down there," Scotty replied, walking toward his shopping cart.

To Trigg's surprise, Sharlene didn't say anything to him. It might have had something to do with the fact that she was fucking Scotty. He didn't care as long as she didn't say shit to him with her stinking ass breath. It only took Scotty fifteen minutes to get Trigg's power back on. Trigg paid him, took his shower, then lay across the bed watching the game until he fell asleep.

Seven

THE NEXT DAY SCHOOL seemed like it was going extra slow for Trigg. He couldn't wait to get out of there so he could get to work. It was free time, and everybody either had a basketball or were watching the girls jump rope. Trigg was sitting on the bleachers by himself thinking about all the money he was about to start making. He was deep in his daydream until he felt someone sit next to him.

"You scared of me, ain't you, Trigg?" Taya asked as she stared into his soul. It was creeping him out the way she looked at him.

"Hell no, I'm not scared of you. I fear no one, remember that. You must have me fucked up with one of these clown-ass niggas, but I handles mine,"

Trigg replied mad that she just tried to play him for a sucker.

She smiled, and it instantly melted away the anger he once was feeling. There was something about Taya that was making Trigg think differently about big girls.

"Can you handle me?" she asked. "From the looks of it, you look a bit too skinny to handle all this woman." She pointed to her body, that even though it was thick, looked very well proportioned.

"Oh, trust me, baby, I can handle you and so much more. The question is, can you handle me? I've been told that I'm the shit, and guess what, I know it," Trigg said smiling, showing all thirty-two of his pearly white teeth.

"It's only one way to find out, right? I mean, unless you're scared," she replied, calling his bluff.

To his surprise, Taya had totally put him in a situation where he needed to step up to the plate or be called a sissy. He was still a virgin and didn't know how to please a woman, except for what he'd seen on television. To top it all off, his boss's sister was the one that was trying to clown him, and he wasn't having that.

"I'm never scared to handle things that need to be handled. Be careful what you wish for 'cause you just might get it."

Those were the last words he said as he got up to go play ball with his friends. As he walked away, Taya called his name. He turned around to see what she wanted.

"Never say never. We gonna find out just how much you can handle, mark my words on that. You can play hard to get, but I'm a get you, and you will be mines," she said, blowing him a kiss as she walked away switching her ass.

Trigg just stared at her ass bouncing back and forth and couldn't take his eyes away. Then unexpectedly, she turned and caught him looking. She just winked her eyes at him and continued walking over to where her friends were jumping rope. Trigg decided he was going to have to call her bluff one day. He just hoped he would be ready.

"Okay, everyone, let's head back to the classroom so I can give out your homework assignments before class is over," the teacher yelled out, causing everyone to stop what they were doing and head back in.

As soon as they received their assignments, the bell rang. Trigg barely even noticed it was time to leave, because he felt too anxious about later. Him and James walked down the hall conversing about different things.

"So you and Wayne coming over my crib later to talk about how everything went the other night, or what? We can play NBA2K 18," James said.

Trigg could barely hear him from the muffled giggles coming from behind them. He looked back, and Taya was right behind them, almost breathing down his neck. Trigg once again got a weird feeling that she wanted to eat him up, but brushed it off with a chuckle.

"I'm not following to you, Tiriq, so don't get all Joe," she said, causing her friends to laugh. Trigg, being quick on his feet, had to counter her smart remark.

"Well that's obvious, being as though we're all heading to the same place, so I would never be Joe ugly."

That stopped all the snickering and laughter they were doing. Tension was now in the air, and was elevating as if some drama was about to start. Taya was the first to start her shit.

"I'm not ugly, lil boy, so fall back, 'cause you wish you had a bad bitch like me, but you don't, do you?" she shot back, putting emphasis on "lil boy."

Trigg laughed because she was so cute when she was mad. That was another plus in his book. He knew he had to play nice with her because he wasn't trying to fuck up what he had going on with her brother.

"Do you know how pretty you are when you're mad?" Trigg stated, then walked away, leaving her standing there with her friends dumbfounded.

"Okay, playa, I see how you handled that," James said as they headed out the door to meet up with

Wayne. "I'm taking notes with your sweet-talking ass."

"That was something light," Trigg replied, spotting Wayne sitting on the hood of somebody's car. "I have to go meet up with big homie, but I will hit your jack later to let you know when we will be linking up, okay?"

"That's cool with me, bro. Talk to you later, and tell Wayne stop fronting like that's his whip he's sitting on."

Trigg ignored that last comment from James and headed over to his friend. They dapped each other up, then started walking down the street to meet up with Moe.

* * *

They arrived at Moe's club just as he was coming outside. He waved them over and told them to get in. Trigg and Wayne hopped inside as all the young bulls stood around watching. They were wishing that it was them about to take a ride in the all-white Phantom Ghost. Moe had just copped it from the federal auction and was showing off in his new toy as if he had just bought it fresh off the lot.

He took them to a store and told them to pick out four sets of clothes, a pair of sneakers, and a pair of Timberland boots. Moe had laced the two young bulls, and now it was time to pay the piper. Once they left the store, he took them to the trap house they were going to be working out of. The place looked like an old rundown building on the outside, but when they opened the door to go inside, it was a whole other world. The place was decked out with used but new furniture. It had an 80-inch plasma screen television on the wall that showed cameras all around the building. No one would be sneaking up on them.

They walked into the kitchen, and both Trigg's and Wayne's eyes got big at the sight of all the dope being cut and bagged up. That wasn't the only thing they saw, either. There were around eight women wearing nothing but thongs, sitting at the table. Moe showed them the other room where four other women were counting stacks and stacks of money. There were guards armed with assault weapons posted in each room.

"These are your new monitors, so get used to seeing them. Anybody gives them a problem, you will have to deal with me," Moe stated, giving them a cold stare.

The whole city was scared of Moe and his team of killers. That was why whatever he wanted to do, he did it with no problem. The only people he really couldn't push around were law enforcement.

"So how do we contact you if we need something?" Trigg asked, sitting on the couch.

"Here," he replied, passing them burner phones. "They are not for personal use, only business, okay?"

They both nodded their heads in agreement, then tucked the phones in their pockets. It was now time to get down to business and get at the money. All they had to do was watch the women cut and bag up the dope, and when the blocks were low, ride with the driver to drop off the new shipment. This was the easiest job they could ever have, but it had its cautions also. They had to watch out for the law and the stickup niggas. The only people that weren't strapped in the building were them and the girls, so they were more than safe there. A motherfucker would be crazy to run up in that place.

"Alright, I'm out of here. I'll hit you up later when it's time to switch shifts. You two will be working together, so no bullshit, got it?" Once again they nodded in agreement. As soon as Moe left, they both high-fived each other and pounded their fists together.

"We fucking on, bro. Let's get this fucking money," Wayne stated excitedly.

"No fucking doubt," Trigg replied, sitting at the table, watching the girls work. His eyes never left this one girl's breasts. He wondered how soft they would be if he squeezed them.

Eight

"HURRY UP, PUSSY-ASS Arab, and empty that fucking register, before I give you something to hesitate about!" Stacks screamed at the trembling man behind the 7-Eleven counter, in Kensington.

Stacks had been on a robbing spree, holding up convenience stores early in the mornings. The stores were randomly picked, so the police had not yet discovered the three men in masks.

"Bitch, I said hurry up!" Stacks barked again, growing very impatient by the ticking seconds.

"Man, I got something to make his ass hurry up!" Gutter yelled as he turned his Glock 40 on one of the store clerks who was lying on the ground.

BOOM! BOOM! BOOM!

"Okay! Okay! Okay! Everything, man, take it!" the Arab screamed in panic after seeing Gutter blow the brains out of his sister-in-law's head.

Gutter was a slim, six foot, brown skin, twenty-two-year-old crazy motherfucker, who was from South Philly. He and Stacks were codefendants on a lot of robberies, and both were made for each other because they complimented one another.

Stacks gathered the money and then prepared to leave the store, when he noticed they were running over on time. On most occasions, the duo was in and out, in under two minutes. Hearing the sirens approaching, Stacks aimed at the Arab's chest and fired.

BOOM! BOOM! BOOM! BOOM! BOOM!

"Let's go!" Stacks shouted, grabbing the bag of money as he stormed out the front door with Gutter on his heels.

They both made the getaway to where their third compadre awaited them behind the wheel of a stolen Dodge Ram pickup. His name was Murda, a superb getaway driver. As soon as the duo hopped inside, half of the police district swarmed the 7-Eleven from a back entrance.

"Roll, Murda!" Stacks yelled to his partner, who smashed on the gas pedal and peeled off into traffic, initiating a chase. The police cruisers immediately pursued the black Dodge Ram, simultaneously calling in the stolen plate numbers.

"Shit!" Stacks exclaimed.

Out of all the damn times they had hit stores and successfully gotten away, a minute too late had caused them to be in the trouble they were in now. Fortunately for them, Murda was an artistic driver when it came to eluding the police in times like this. He swiftly maneuvered through traffic, running red lights at intersections, and caused a wreck behind him.

Damn! That nigga sure knows how to handle that wheel! Stacks thought as he held onto the support bar above his head.

"Shoot 'em off so I can duck us off!" Murda shouted.

Without any reluctance, Stacks dropped his window and grabbed a MAC-10 that was resting on the passenger floor for backup. He racked it and then sat out the window. While holding on to the support bar with his right hand, he simultaneously fired at the pursuing police cruisers, causing them to swerve and wreck. Gutter pulled back the Ram's sliding back window and stuck his twin Glock 40s out and participated in the fusillade. Every police cruiser that came in view was knocked off by the duo.

Murda made a right onto Delaware Ave, and vigorously accelerated through more traffic lights. When the trio made it to I-95, Murda turned right and then abruptly made a U-turn, causing Stacks to almost lose control, but he held onto the bar like a raging bull's ropes.

"We about to dump!" Murda said as he turned into a public store parking lot, upsetting cruisers who were trapped in the wreckage behind them.

The trio quickly exited the truck and carjacked the first occupied vehicle they saw turning toward the highway. Murda pulled the old woman from the driver's seat of the Dodge Caravan and blew her brains from her head.

BOOM! BOOM! No witnesses.

Murda put the Caravan in drive and inconspicuously drove away from the scene, in the opposite direction. They didn't want to jump on the highway because they could easily get caught, so they took the back roads. He quickly made his way to the first I-76 ramp he could find, and headed toward South Philly.

Damn! That was close, Stacks thought as they drove in silence down the expressway. Gutter sparked up the loud, and they enjoyed the weed all the way to the spot.

* * *

"Hey, Trigg, hold on for a second. I have to ask you something important."

He didn't even have to turn around to know who it was calling him. He knew her voice from anywhere. When she caught up to him, Trigg smiled at her.

"What's up with you, little mama. What can I do for your sexy ass?"

"Oh, you can do a lot for me, you just don't know it yet. Do you want to come over to my house? My mom's still at work and we can have some quality time alone to get to know each other," she said, smiling seductively.

"What time do your mom get home from work?"

"Well we got out early today and I never told her, so she thinks it's a full day of school. She won't be home till 3:30 or 4:00 this evening. So does that mean you coming, because we really need to get to our likes and dislikes to better understand each other."

It wasn't what she said, it's how she said it that made it sound so lustful. Trigg was turned on by the way she said it and really wanted to go to her crib with her but was scared that her brother would just pop up. After thinking about it for a second he thought to himself, *Fuck it, why not?*

"Yeah, I'll go with you. Why not? Just hold up for a second and let me tell my man that I'll catch up with him later on. Oh yeah, by the way, he likes Sarah, so try to hook that up for him."

"Um, only if you knew, but she do think he's cute, so I'll put in the work for him," Taya replied.

"Ard, give me about five minutes, and then we'll be out, okay?" Trigg said, heading over toward where Wayne and James were standing.

"No problem, but don't take too long. I got some things I would like to do," she responded it in a seductive voice. Trigg couldn't do anything but smile. He was wondering if she was still a virgin.

As is he walked over to where Wayne and James were standing, he noticed that Wayne was already talking to Sarah and they were laughing and giggling with each other. He approached them and shook Wayne's hand then looked at Sarah.

"What's up, Sarah?"

"The question is, what's up with you and my girl Tay? Don't be acting stupid with her. She's a good girl. She's really feeling you, so don't fuck it up."

"Chill, I got shorty. She's going to be alright. We're about to roll to her crib anyway and chill for a few minutes. That's what I was coming over here to tell my man, so don't worry about what we doing," he shot back sarcastically.

The look on her face was priceless. Trigg knew he finally was able to get up under her skin. He just couldn't believe how easy it was to make her mad.

To calm her down a bit, he just faked like he was about to punch her in the arm, and she started to smile.

"You know I was only playing with you. I would never do anything to that girl, but on some real shit, homes, I'm going to check you later 'cause I have to go."

Just as he started walking down the street he heard someone calling his name. He didn't want to turn around because he didn't know who was calling him. All he did know was that it was a female's voice. He looked over in that direction to see who it was.

Trigg's heart started beating fast. It was the chick from the other night at the club when they first went inside to talk to Moe. She was rocking a cream-color Christian Dior three-button blouse, a pair of baby-blue skinny leg Seven jeans, and a pair of high heels. Her nails were done and her hair was wrapped in an elegant bun showing off her natural beautiful features. She was pushing a smoke-gray Porsche Panamera, and looked even more beautiful than he had seen before.

"Come here right now. I know you heard me calling you. Your mother's going to be furious with you when I tell her you were ignoring your auntie. What, are you showing off in front of your girlfriend or something? Now get in this car, boy, and hurry up," she stated with her hands on her hips.

At first he was lost, and you could see the perplexity on his face, but then recognition settled in and he smiled. She returned the gesture, and instantly his little man started smiling too.

"Who that?" Sarah asked, looking for confirmation from one of them.

"That's my aunt right there on my dad side," he said. "They all are crazy."

"Oh, well tell her you're walking me home and you will see her later." Tay stood obstinately with her arms folded.

Just as he was about to say something else someone tapped him on the shoulder. When he turned around it was the girl standing there gorgeously with her hands on her hips smiling. Trigg almost fainted. She was everything he could ever imagine, and it was doubtful that he would ever be able to get someone of her caliber. Now here he was standing in front of her and also the chick that he was supposed to go back to the crib with. He had to quickly decide who he would be going with, and fast, because this was his first time ever having to choose between two women.

"Listen, I have to go with my aunt right now, but I will hit you up later on and we can chill then. Is that cool with you?"

Taya looked at him disappointedly, but then the disappointment eased up because she knew it was out of his control that he had to go with his family right now. She definitely planned on seeing him at another time, though, and she was going to really hold it to him. He started walking toward the chick's car. Deep down inside he was smiling from ear to ear knowing that he made the right decision.

"So I guess that means we can get up out of here now, huh? Oh yeah, and don't worry about calling her later, because you're going to be too busy," the chick stated, getting into the car.

"Busy doing what?" Trigg asked suspiciously.

"How did you know where my school was anyway?"

"That was easy to find because there are only a few schools around your area, and plus I didn't know. I just seen you coming out and walking with that girl, and I got jealous, so I decided to come over there and intervene. I'm glad that I did because you probably would have been missing out on something good," she said, licking her lips.

"You are so bad, but I like that."

"You can beat me for it later, and don't flatter yourself, but Moe told me everything about you. He also told me to take you shopping and show you a good time. Then he wants to see you and Wayne, so chop, chop; we have a busy day and I know you'll enjoy yourself, maybe even more than me. We'll just pick something out for Wayne while we're out, and you can give it to him when we snatch him up on the way back," she said, blowing him a kiss. For the first time in his little life, Trigg was in love.

"Is this your car?" Trigg asked, looking around inside the Porsche. It was one of the baddest cars he had ever seen in a long time, and when she took off, it flew down the street. He couldn't believe how fast the car was.

"It's mine. You didn't see my name on the license plate before you got in? Cutie, you better start paying more attention and being more observant of your surroundings. That will be one of the keys to your success in this business that you want to be involved in so much. I just hope you're ready."

"I was born ready. You will see that sooner or later. I hope you're ready for it."

"I sure hope so. That remains to be seen," she said, pulling out into traffic.

They drove around to so many different stores and picked out so many clothes for both him and Wayne. Trigg now possessed five pairs of Jordans. That was more than he ever possessed in his whole life. After collecting all of the clothes, they picked Wayne up and headed over to talk to their boss. The meeting didn't last long because they had to get over to the trap house and work. Things were starting to look up for the two young boys, or so they thought.

Nine

PARKED TWO DOORS DOWN from their target house in the upscale suburban neighborhood of Northeast Philadelphia, Shy and a couple of his goons were growing restless and were ready to make their move. According to his assessment it was supposed to be an easy come-up, but one could never be too sure with the clown they were after. A smooth talker who always had an ulterior motive, it was oftentimes tough to determine what exactly an easy come-up consisted of.

"My nigga, what made you even think, let alone feel, like stealing this old as car to do this job with, man?" Smoke asked, referring to the beat-up older model Ford Taurus they were sitting in.

"Man, you always complaining. At least I came through and found something for us, unlike those niggas you were dealing with the other night who stole that dumbass car and it was slow as hell. We were lucky to get out of that thing unscathed," Murder yelled. It didn't really matter to him what they were in. The goal was getting to the money, and that was what they were about to do.

"Yo, I got a bad feeling about this," Shy hesitantly admitted, heading to the meaningless chatter and the smoked-out stolen vehicle they were in. He didn't want to admit he was getting cold feet, but they had been sitting there for hours, and he was growing more nervous each and every second they wasted staying stagnant in the same spot.

Turning up his nose and turning around to face Shy, who was in the backseat, Drama took a quick pull from his tightly rolled blunt and passed it to the back.

"Nigga, take that shit and calm your fucking nerves. Let me find out this bitch nigga scared," Wu said to the rest of the team, with a throaty laugh as he coughed smoke out of his mouth into his hands. The loud was too much for his lungs to bear.

Facing the joking, Shy grew serious. He was the oldest and often felt like the leader of the two. Joke time was over and he was ready to move out; there was no time to show weakness.

"Naw, awesome, real shit. Everything's good, my nigga. We're just going to get in and get out. Ain't no time for the weak shit. That'll get niggas killed—or worse, booked." To Wu, getting locked up was worse than death.

"I hear you. Chill the fuck out. I'm good," Shy

responded quietly, while taking in an extralong pull from the blunt to help calm his rattling nerves.

Peering around nervously, Shy couldn't seem to get a grip on his racing thoughts. Running into this particular house was one thing, but crossing his father was another. He knew when it was all said and done, there was going to be extreme consequences for his actions and what was about assume transpire. He did his best to shake that feeling, as it was too late to turn back now. Besides, the loud he had been smoking was quickly taking effect, and the "fuck it" attitude was kicking in.

"What if there're more people in the crib and they have guns?" Shy asked seriously, thinking more deeply into if things went wrong.

Finally chiming in, Turk responded this time, "Nigga, we went over this shit a hundred times." He was growing frustrated with Shy and his hesitance. He was well aware of why he and Wu had befriended these dudes. He was the son of big Moe, a heavy hitter in the hood, supplying over 69 percent of the drugs flooding the streets. However, times like this, he would often grow annoyed and lose his patience with him. "It's just him and his bitch, just like you said. We've been laying on this nigga for over a week now; we should be good. Now stop asking dumb-ass questions and let's go get this money."

"Yeah, what's up with you?" Wu sighed deeply. He too had enough of the scared acting shit. "You know this nigga better than us and you are starting to make us question your G status."

Smacking his teeth, Shy quickly shot back, "Nigga, stop playing with me. You know I'm about that life. Matter of fact, fuck all this talking; let's go," he stated, doing his best to sound like a gangster. He didn't want to look like a sucker in front of his niggas, and even worse, appear soft. Street money raised him, and in his mind, he was born and bred for this shit. After all, he was born into this light and he proved himself time and time again in the past.

Wu was good at pushing people's buttons and instigating. He was also good at manipulating people. Shy was so desperate to be like his friends. In reality, they were like night to his day. They never understood why a privileged kid like him tried so hard to imitate the scumbag trash that they had unfortunately grown up to be.

Despite knowing that Shy was basically selling his soul to fit in, Wu proceeded with their plan to capitalize off his desire for acceptance.

Displaying his full set of teeth, Shy looked at Wu

and stated, "Let's get this money."

With their black ski masks on, the trio made their way out of the car and scurried onto the dark, deserted streets. To their advantage, residents of the wealthy community had retired to their beds and were oblivious to the horror that would soon take place right on their streets.

Shy led the pack away from the front, then to the back door where he knew they would have easy access to the lavish but lightly secure home. He had been there many times as a boy with his father and knew the drug kingpin personally.

They quickly crept along the side of the house. The idea was to remain undetected. Once arriving at the back door, Shy slowly and carefully turned the knob on the back door to check and see if it was already open. It wasn't. Shy, who was still nervous, looked over to Wu and gave him a head nod that meant to proceed. Bubbling with excitement, Wu came up and pulled his concealed crowbar from the inside of his coat. He lined it up and pried it along the door panel. He held up his gloved hand and used his fingers to silently count to three. It was now or never.

Using his shoulder to press against the door, he pulled the crowbar simultaneously until the wood cracked and the door popped open. It was go time, and everyone was ready.

The blaring sound of the alarm caused Jose to jump out of his sleep. Snatching back the luxurious sheet set from his pajama-clad body, he immediately went to reach over and grab his 9 mm from his nightstand. If he had to shoot, he wanted to be able to do so quickly. Before he could touch the Italian brass knob on his nightstand, he felt a gun firmly pressed to his forehead.

"Reach and I squeeze," Wu snarled, clutching his .40 cal. tightly. "Now we going to do this my way. You're going to get up and deactivate that alarm you have on. If you do as I say, no one gets hurt, but if you try some dumb shit, I'll rock everybody in this bitch to sleep. Get up," he demanded.

Wu wasn't new to home invasion. He knew he had about sixty seconds to stop the alarm before police were notified. It was surprising; as much money as Jose was allegedly getting, his security system was bullshit. He was barely a step up from ADT. He didn't even have any of his henchmen hanging around the house like kingpins usually did.

Wu backed away slowly and cautiously, to make room and allow Jose to get up. Because Wu's eyes were struggling to adjust to the dark, Jose led the way. Wu quickly followed him to the front door, where he proceeded to deactivate the alarm. As Wu walked off, Shy and Turk hit the lights to find something to tie up Jose and his wife, Alexia.

Wu quickly tore through the closet and found a few long-sleeve shirts. "Tie that bitch up. I'm 'bout to search this motherfucker."

As Shy did as he was told, Wu and Turk walked back into the room. Jose appeared deathly calm; however, no one could mistake the anger in his demeanor. Noticing the blatant hostility, Wu turned around and walked over to him. He withdrew his gun from his waistband and violently smacked Jose across the face with it. No attitudes were allowed. The fact he even had one was an insult. He should have been grateful he was still breathing.

His knees buckled from the blow, and pain shot through the top half of his body, but Jose refused to cry out. Witnessing the assault, Alexia screamed out.

"Please, God! No, don't hurt him, please!" she cried, in a fit of panic.

Shy I immediately grabbed her by the throat and squeezed. "Bitch, shut the fuck up with all that yelling!" he said, before shoving her to the bed.

Taking control of the situation so they could hurry up and get the fuck out of there, Wu spoke. "I'm only gonna ask one time. Where's the fucking money and work? I'm not leaving without it. It's either going to be with your shit or with your life. Starting with that loud-ass bitch of yours," he said, using his gun to point to Alexia, who was laid out on the bed tied up. "Now I'm going to gag her to silence her screams."

She appeared paralyzed with fear, and her face was soaked from the constant flow of tears from her eyes. Wu didn't care. He didn't have time for games and theatrics.

Shy had told them that Jose was a heavy hitter in the city and that it would be easy to just take his shit so he couldn't supply his workers or other dealers that were using him as a plug. Still in pain and equally terrified, Jose didn't hesitate to point to the closet. He lived and breathed for his family, and they were worth more to him than some dirty money. They could have the couple hundred grand in his trunk. He could have it back in no time.

"It's in the closet, underneath the shoes. The big black trunk. Keys are in the top drawer over there," he stated quickly, while pointing to the dresser. He was still holding his face, blood oozing through the cracks of his fingers.

Jose was clearly outnumbered, and he wasn't about to put up a fight. He just wanted them to take what they needed and get the fuck out. He figured they weren't there to kill him since they had on the masks. He knew the saying all too well: "When they're masked up, they're coming for your ice. If they're bare faced, they're coming for your life." He cursed himself for not having more security on tonight. That would never happen again though.

With dollar signs in his eyes, Wu waved for Turk to hit the closet and open the trunk. Pushing Jose onto the bed beside his wife, he yanked the silk case off of a pillow and shoved it into Jose's mouth. Even though he was restrained, Jose wasted no time trying to consult Alexia. He remained silent as he rubbed his face against hers, silently ensuring that everything would be okay.

Turk snatched open the top drawer to the dresser Jose had pointed to, and retrieved the simple small brown key to the trunk. They had been expecting a safe and were delighted by how easy the night was turning out to be.

"Yo, make sure that bitch tied up good, and then go search the rest of the crib. We got three minutes and then we out," he instructed Shy.

Shy looked irritated by Wu's request, but once again did as he was told. He wanted to be the one to hit the stash because it was his drop. Wu and Turk were his niggas, but he wanted to make sure they split the come-up evenly down the middle. He was younger than the both of them, and at times he felt like they tried to treat him like a sucker. Nevertheless, Shy made sure Alexia was secure, and began to head out of the room.

Over in the closet, Turk's eyes lit up like a Christmas tree when he was saw the old green trunk safely nestled underneath the dozen rows of designer shoes. With excitement fueling him, he inserted the key into the chamber.

Before he could push open the heavy top to the chest, the faint sound of a door swinging, along with subsequent running down the hall, stopped him in his tracks. The sound coming from the pitch-black hallway also caused Shy to stop abruptly as he was walking out of the room to search the rest of the large house. Wu, who had been standing by the bed next to Jose, also appeared stunned by the noise. As the sound neared, Alexia and Jose started to squirm, wiggle, and shake to get out of their restraints. Their muffled attempts to yell caused Wu and Shy to grow alarmed. Someone else was in the house, but it was too dark to see who it was and what they were carrying.

The rapid footsteps grew dangerously close; then a shadow appeared by the door. Fear gripped Shy, and without thinking, he frantically drew his gun. Before Wu could yell for him to wait, he fired through the door. The running immediately stopped, and the sound of a body hitting the floor could be heard. Shy lowered his gun and the image was clearer, the shadow and person now visible.

"Shit," Shy cried out, with panic flooding him. They were all fucked.

Ten

"YOU CAN'T TELL ME who I can and can't hang with. Those are my niggas, and besides, you act like you didn't grow up doing the same shit. This is the same game that made you who you are today," Wayne argued with his father, who was growing increasingly irritated with every word Wayne uttered. "That's some real, live, hypocritical shit," Wayne continued.

"Who the fuck you think you talking to? Don't get fucked up in here!" Jay threatened angrily while rapidly approaching his son with clenched teeth and tight fists. He felt he was being challenged, and he was about to give Wayne something he wasn't quite ready for.

"As long as you live in my fucking house, you gonna do what the fuck I tell you to do. You know, you really sound fucking stupid. Yeah, those streets made me, but they didn't make you. You have no idea what I've been through to get here, to give you and your sister a decent life. You're a fake-ass thug and you're going to wind up getting hurt. Although my name is strong in the streets, that alone don't mean shit to these other niggas out here trying to make a quick come-up. You think your little friends fuck with you on the strength of you? If you do, you're dumber than I thought!" he yelled at his son, trying to reason with him.

"Whatever, I'm not going to argue with you," Wayne muttered angrily, before walking away and making his way to his room. He had pissed his father off big-time, and he wasn't about to make him even angrier by continuing to argue with him. He was out of there. Wayne figured if push came to shove, he would just move in with Trigg.

In the past few months Trigg and Wayne had been killing the game. Moe had trusted them with all of the stash spots now, and they were the major two young boys on the streets. Giving them gifts and anything they, he treated them like they were his kids. Trigg stayed by himself in his crib, and he had decked it out even better than what it was. That was like the new hangout spot for him and his squad that he formed. After Wayne packed up a lot of his clothes and stuff, he waited for his father to go to sleep before taking everything over to his friend's house. He already knew that it would be cool for him to stay there because Trigg already had been trying to get him to come over there. Now they were united and were going to party all night long.

"Man, you are crazy for talking to your pops like that," Trigg stated as they made their rounds, collecting money.

"Man, it was time for me to get up out of there anyway. I'm about to be eighteen soon, and they were going to kick me out anyway, so fuck it," Wayne replied.

"After we grab the rest of the money, we have to take it over to Moe because he has to meet up with Jose today."

"Didn't he say we would do that?"

"That was the original plan, but Jose insisted on seeing him personally. We're still going with him though. Go ahead and grab the shit while I find somewhere to park," Trigg said, pulling over.

Ever since even messing with Na'tae, he had

been driving her whip. She had taught both of them how to drive and even helped him get his junior driver's license. She even helped with school and the rules to the game, giving him the raw and uncut version no one else would give him. The only thing that she asked from him was that he never cross the team. She didn't even care if he went out and fucked other girls. As long as he continued to give her the dick, she didn't mind at all. She continued to strip at the club, but she also enjoyed spending Trigg's money. That was the small price he had to pay for getting that pussy.

* * *

When Jay woke up and saw that his son was gone, he knew he had lost him to the streets, just like his own father had done with him. He kind of blamed himself for spoiling Wayne as a child. Since the tender age of seventeen when he found out his girl Bella was pregnant. Jay had done his absolute best to ensure that his family would want for nothing. Before the piss could dry on the pregnancy test, he started making moves. He hustled hard by pushing packs on the corner, running his own blocks, and ultimately running nearly the entirety of West Philly. That alone was a milestone for someone like Jay, who grew up poor with no decent role models and only the hustlers to look up to.

Landing on top didn't come without its fair share of bloodshed. Working for niggas was never a long-term option for him, so when he found out his only choices were to either push packs directly for the block runners or pay them to hustle on the block, he chose the latter. To him it didn't matter, since within months he was running down on the runners and taking over the blocks. A lot of niggas had come up missing during his five-year rise, even suppliers.

To him, only the strong survive and deserve to be on top. This takeover method worked in every aspect of his hustle, and now at the age of thirty-eight, most of the dope that was sold in Philly came from him. It had been that way for nearly sixteen years.

With the lifestyle he lived, he knew his family would be vulnerable. With his dedication to his family fueling him, he saved diligently and moved his family to the best area he could afford. While his daughter appreciated it and embraced the life they lived, his son resented it because of the unglamorous boredom and normalcy. It didn't help that in his younger and less intelligent days, he would often take a young and highly impressionable Wayne with him during runs to the hood. Cash, flying cars, and pretty women were the norm to the boy. He admired his father's power and yearned to emulate his infamy on the streets of Philadelphia.

As Jay grew older, he grew wiser and purposely shielded his children from the dangerous lifestyle. However, it was a little too late. It didn't matter to Wayne that Jay had established a legitimate family landscaping and property business so they could have something for themselves. It was very modest money compared to what he had seen in the drug world, but it was a lot more than what most people had. They literally wanted for nothing, and his kids even had trust funds tucked away and waiting for them when they reached twenty-five.

In Jay's mind his children were above the cold streets he was bred in. He envisioned Wayne as a future entrepreneur, not some fake-ass wannabe.

Wayne was by no means a thug in any form. He would easily be considered a sheep in the street, food, or prey, someone who was weak and vulnerable. To say he was privileged was an understatement. His typical attire included $100 button-ups and $400 Giuseppes. That was one of the reasons Wayne always let his friend hold his sneaks or clothes. He was a suburban kid whose only tie to the hood was his father. Jay knew Wayne name-dropped every chance he got. His son was a follower who had been brainwashed by the false glamorization of the streets, and his friend who persuade him into going into the business.

Jay knew without a doubt that if Wayne were put in the wrong situation, the average cat would chew him up and spit him out. He would do everything in his power to prevent that from happening. He knew he wasn't going to always be around to save him, so he would do his best to keep him out of the hood and away from the wolves he called his friends. It was actually too late for that because Wayne was already out there and there was no turning back now.

Wayne's parents decided to let him go since he had already left. If he wanted to learn the hard way, then they had no choice but to let him. After checking his room and seeing that he had left and taken a lot of his clothes, Jay went downstairs and inform the rest of his family that his son had left to be on his own. Bella was mad, but she understood because she stood by her man the whole time that he did his thing, so one thing for certain, two things for sure, she knew that Wayne would come home sooner or later and that she would still take him in with open arms.

Eleven

"I HAVE A QUESTION for you," Trigg said as he and Na'Tae lay in bed together, after having sex for the second time that night. "Did you and Moe ever, you know, have sex?"

"Fucked? No, he's like a father to me. All he wants is my loyalty, and he's got that until the day I die." The look she gave him said it all, and he knew from that point on that he had her all to himself.

"Sorry I asked that question, but I just needed to know. He's like a father to me also, and I'm going to do whatever I can to make sure he knows that he can trust me through whatever comes our way. From what I see this is a shady business and you have to be on point at all times."

"I know that. Moe also knows how risky this shit is, but he's still on top after all this time, and believe me, he's not going anywhere," Na'Tae replied, getting dressed. She was playing a role to see if she would be able to trust him when the time was right. Moe's time was ticking in the game, and she needed someone she would be able to mold into position. That was one of the reasons why when Moe asked her to take care of Trigg, she jumped at the opportunity. She also saw the potential in him. "Hurry up and get dressed. We have some shit to do."

"Where are we going?"

"To handle some shit over at one of the trap houses," Na'Tae replied.

"Cool, let's roll then," Trigg said, quickly getting ready. He grabbed his burner from under the pillow and stuck it underneath his shirt. Na'Tae just smiled.

As they were walking out of the crib, Trigg noticed a couple of niggas gambling in front of the door. They had so much money on the ground that it looked like the ground was made of money. Trigg looked at Na'Tae, and she smiled 'cause she already knew what he was thinking. He loved playing craps and would win all the time. He wanted to see if he could get some of that free money from them.

"Man, shake the fucking dice. You ain't gone keep sticking every fucking number. Fuck you think, this paper grow on trees? Niggas dying for less and living for more," DJ stated, growing frustrated. Him and a group of young hustlers were gambling because there was nothing else to do.

"Kev, these peanuts. Fuck you down, ten thousand? I just brought my bitch that new Bentley GTC cherry red for two hundred. Youngin' I could give a flying fuck about you getting frustrated over my shot. Stop what you don't like or you deserve to get stuck, you fucking young vic."

"Old head ain't gone be to many more vics, nuts, or anything else that come out your slick-ass mouth, I'm telling you now," DJ stated.

"Young nigga, you are and will be any fucking thing I say you are. Right now you my vic. My boo needs Gucci bags and Chanel shoes, so pussy gets daddy's money. Now eight dice, gator boots. That's it right there. Get my money, sucker," he shouted.

While Slim was on the ground talking slick, DJ was over his head making finger gun gestures for lil Mike to go get the hammer off the car tire. Kev never saw Mike pass DJ the chrome .357 Magnum.

"Damn old head, I had enough for one day. I can't take no more. Please, man, stop the bleeding.

Here go your paper right here. I'm copping out."

"Damn, I knew you young niggas was sweet and soft, but I wasn't expecting big bad DJ to do no copping out, especially over some paper. But then again, sometimes you have to expect the unexpected."

That's exactly what happened as Slim looked up into the barrel of DJ's cannon as he held it to the side of his head.

Trigg and Na'Tae were walking toward them until they saw the gun come out. They quickly turned around and headed back toward the house in a hurry.

"Come on, young buck, not like this. That's Hustler Talk 101 in gambling," Slim stated, shitting bricks at the size of DJ's Magnum. You never would expect to see that look on Slim's face.

"Man, push that fucking paper back across and

stop bitching."

"Alright, alright, chill, youngin'. It's all their money."

"Naw, this is all their money."

BOOM! BOOM! BOOM!

The three slugs from the chrome .357 Magnum knocked Slim's brains right out of his head and all over his Jordan sneakers. Brain fragments were on DJ's face. Still in monster mode, once Slim's body collapsed to the ground, DJ stood over his body and fired away.

BOOM! BOOM! BOOM!

* * *

"Carlos! *Hola mi amigo. Como estas?*" Moe asked, while smiling brightly as he gave him a strong handshake, before immediately inviting him into his home.

"I'm doing okay, Moe," Carlos responded with a smile. Moe always greeted him with Spanish words in a jovial manner. Carlos suspected it had a lot to do with the amount of work he had been serving to him and his team. He was surprised that he ran through all that dope so fast.

They had been doing business for a long time now, and their bond had grown to that of more than just business associates.

"Just okay?" Carlos asked, while barring two rows of perfectly aligned, shiny white teeth, perfected by an orthodontist. "As much money as you make you should be doing great!" he said, with a hearty laugh and in a thick accent. "Come!" he gestured with his hands.

Following Carlos through the palatial space, Moe couldn't help but admire the intricate Spanish details of the lovely home he religiously visited twice a month.

The contemporary Mediterranean stucco style home, custom designed by Carlos's wife, Alexia, was a staple in her country, solidifying one's wealthy status. Growing up poor in Guadalajara, Alexia would often dream of living in one of the homes her mother used to clean tirelessly. She and Carlos had been together for over twenty years, and every chance he got, he strived to make each and every one of her dreams come true.

"Come sit down," Carlos said, ushering Moe into his lavish office at the back of his home. Moe took a seat onto the leather couch across from Carlos's large, executive style, cherry wood desk. He wasn't nervous, but felt a bit uneasy being without his burner. He did his best to make himself comfortable.

Taking a seat, Carlos retrieved a Cuban cigar from his drawer, lit it, and took a long drag from it.

"Care for one?" he asked. He already knew the answer. Moe took pride in his physique and refused to pollute his body with any kind of toxins such as alcohol, drugs, or smoke, even though he still smoked weed and took a few sips once in a while.

"No thanks."

"Okay, can I get you anything at all? Something to drink? I can have Alexia make you a plate of paella. She just cooked it. It's delicious," he bragged.

Alexia definitely knew her way around the kitchen, and Moe had tasted some of her delicious creations on multiple occasions.

"I'm good, Carlos, but thank you." Carlos shrugged and took another pull from his cigar. A thick stream of smoke escaped from his lips as he exhaled.

"So what brings you here, my friend?" Carlos asked. "He knew the Moe wouldn't have any money for him until next week. He was early for his shipment and he hoped his premature arrival was for positive reasons. However, he wasn't so sure. Moe seemed distant, and it appeared something was bothering him.

"Well, I wanted to talk to you about something important," Moe said with a sigh before pausing. It was now or never, and he wasn't quite sure how it was going to go.

"Speak, my friend. What troubles you?" he asked, leaning back in his desk chair. His eyes pierced deeply into Moe's and revealed his curiosity.

"I don't know how to say this, Carlos, but I'm ready to give this shit up and pass the torch to my lil homie," he admitted, silently breathing a sigh of relief.

It had come out easier than he thought it would.

"You want out?" Carlos asked, pausing. He was confused, and Moe now had his full attention.

"You mean you want out of the game, this lifestyle?" he asked for clarification.

"Yeah," Moe responded, making eye contact with his connect.

"I don't know what to say. In my country, the only way out is death."

Moe swallowed hard but stood his ground through eye contact. He wasn't scared of a fucking soul, so whatever he was going to do, he better do it now before Carlos got him.

"Hopefully that is not the case here. I've been in this game for nearly twenty years. I've made you a lot of money. Money that enabled you to provide a beautiful life for your family. Right now my family requires my full attention. I have a daughter about to college, a growing business, and a wife that is going to either drive me out of business or wind up taking it all if I don't step up and get out. Earlier today, I met with a friend, one I've known and done business with for over five years, one I considered my friend. That same friend is under secret surveillance and tried to set me up." Moe sighed. "You see, Carlos, my time is winding down. All the signs are there. My only choice now is to bow out gracefully or let the streets take me and my family under."

Carlos said nothing. He sat stone faced and quietly stared at Moe. This wasn't the news he was expecting, and he was extremely disappointed in Moe's revelations. Nevertheless, he could tell he was sincere and was deeply troubled. Carlos looked away briefly as he took his cigar and put it out in a nearby glass ashtray. Directing his icy gaze back to Moe, he continued to sit quietly. Moe wondered what Carlos was thinking as he stared at him. He hoped and prayed that their conversation wouldn't go left.

"Moe, you're one of my best clients. You make me a lot of money. However, you're not just my client. You are my friend. If you want out then you have my blessing. Family is the most important thing in life; after all, we do this for them." Carlos chuckled, and it instantly lightened the mood of the room.

Moe had him thinking that something larger was troubling him. Carlos had groomed Moe for many years, and while he hoped that he would never stop ruling the streets, he understood his desire to retreat.

Besides, he still had his young and hungry young bull Trigg, who was more than eager to someday fill his spot as the largest supplier in the city.

"Thanks, Carlos. I definitely appreciate it. You've done a lot for me to even be able to get to this point, and for that I thank you."

"Of course, of course," Carlos responded modestly. Carlos had taken Moe under his wing at twenty-two when he was a gun-toting livewire.

He'd heard about the youngster along with his ruthless reputation of having several bodies on his belt. Initially Carlos was hesitant, but after some time, Moe grew on him. He was ambitious, honest, and loyal to a fault. Over the years he'd resolved many issues for Carlos, some peacefully, and some through gunfire. He was one of his best men, and while sad to see him depart, Carlos was happy that he had found a legitimate path to embark upon.

"Do you still want the upcoming load?" Carlos asked.

"Yeah, that'll be my last one and I'm done."

"Fair enough," Carlos stated before getting up from his desk. "Same time, same amount?" he asked.

"Cool," Moe responded, before standing up and preparing to depart the room.

"You can stay a while and enjoy the festivities if you like," Carlos said pointing toward the half-naked women roaming freely around the room.

"Maybe some other time, my friend." Moe walked out the door smiling because he knew that he had just escaped death.

* * *

"Nobody fucking move," Drama screamed, after kicking in the front door with his .45 drawn. Kev was right behind him, while Shy acted as the lookout from outside.

"Ahhhh!" screamed a brown-skinned girl that was crouched over the young man who now sat wide eyed in fear.

Both had been caught off guard, and the girl now quickly scrambled across the ground, on her knees in terror. She disregarded the ring of saliva that had formed around her mouth and seeped onto her shirt from her oral escapade that had been abruptly interrupted by the masked gunmen.

"Where's the money and work? I want everything, and I want it now," Drama demanded.

He wasn't playing, and Dante could tell that, judging by his demeanor. The only thing he could see in the dimly lit house was the homicidal scowl Drama wore on his semi-masked face, and the big black gun that was aimed at his head. Dante wasn't ready to die, and he grew angry that the dude Paco he was working under had him posted up in the stash spot with no muscle. To make matters worse, Paco had picked up earlier than usual, and there was nothing in the house worth taking. He prayed the lack of come-up for the robbers didn't entice them to kill him.

"It's in the back bedroom," he replied calmly. "Open the air-conditioner and you'll find it."

Moving from behind Drama, Kev scurried to the back of the house to find the treasure they had come for. He tucked his gun against his waist. He knew there was no one else in the house but Dante and the jump-off. They had been watching the crib for several days and knew that Monster often left him alone.

"That's what I'm talking 'bout," Drama said, while keeping his gun aimed at Dante.

He wasn't worried about the bitch. She was part of the setup. She knew they were coming; she just wasn't sure what time they would be there. Shy knew her sister, who in turn had convinced her to get back with Dante after he had whooped her ass a few days ago. She would get her cut later. After several tense minutes, Kev returned with a scowl on his face. Handing over the small stack of money to Drama, he turned to face Dante.

"What the fuck is this, nigga?" Drama asked, disgusted. He didn't even bother to count it, as he knew it couldn't have been more than $1,500. They had been expecting at least $5,000 in the house.

"That's all that's there. The big homie picked up earlier," Dante responded, growing increasingly nervous. He was starting to sweat, so he began to say a silent prayer asking the Lord for protection.

"I'm 'bout to pop this nigga and that bitch," Kev stated angrily. He reached in his waist to retrieve his gun.

"Chill," Drama stated firmly before grabbing Rum's arm.

"Fuck that shit!" Kev argued. "I don't have time for fucking games!" He was angry.

They had been expecting much more since the girl Shy was dealing with had bragged that they kept racks in the house in plain view. The $1,500 they actually found was a far cry from what she had been promoting.

"Let the bitch and the little nigga be. No need to catch no body over this shit," Drama, said. "It's still a come-up."

They were still leaving with more than they came with. Disappointed, Kev smacked his teeth but stuffed his gun back in his jeans. He was angry, but ultimately agreed with his cousin. It was Dante's lucky day.

"Tape them the fuck up though so we can get the fuck outta here," Drama demanded, looking at Dante and then over at the girl.

There was no need to waste any more time. Kev grabbed the duct tape out of his back pocket and did as he was told. Taping them up would give them time to flee the scene before anyone knew what happened. By the time someone found them, they would be long gone.

Twelve

THE VIEW FROM THE window of The Chateau was nothing short of stunning. It was exactly what Moe wanted, and he had gone out of his way to make sure he got the perfect table for his daughter's eighteenth birthday.

"Thank you so much, Daddy. I really love it," Taya beamed as she looked out the window and admired the view.

Their seats were right near the window so she could see the water. The lights illuminating from the tall buildings downtown cast an exotic glow on the still, black-like water.

"Anytime," he smiled back. Money was no issue when it came to his baby girl. The three-month advance reservations had set him back a grand, but it was worth every penny.

"And thank you for the bracelet, Kev. It's beautiful." She smiled before glancing down at her 14k gold euro coin bracelet.

Kev nodded. He was happy she liked it. He had just picked it up at the last minute, and it had cost him every cent of the $500 he had gotten off the last-minute West Side caper. Moe smiled before stuffing a forkful of seared porterhouse steak into his mouth. He had another gift for Taya.

"Baby girl, so I wanted to talk to you both about something. Next week I'll be focusing on the business 100 percent." Taya dropped her fork and smiled brightly.

"Oh, Daddy, that's great!" She had longed for the day she would hear the words that he would be exiting the drug game.

The admission caught Kev's attention, causing him to sit straight up. If his partner was moving to the side, then he knew he would be passing the throne down to him. He was ready to take the game to a whole other level.

"So remember the building we saw when we rode downtown. Right near the park?" Moe asked the two of them. "We rode by there the other day and it had the For Lease sign up," Moe continued, trying to refresh their memory.

"Yeah," they replied in unison.

"Well I just signed a five-year lease today." He smiled.

"Daddy, that's awesome!" Taya squealed while literally bouncing up and down.

"So does this mean I get a new office?" she

asked.

"You not only get your own office, but you also get the new title of director of Morgan Enterprises."

"Thank you, Daddy!" she gushed as she scooted from her seat and gave him a big hug.

She was honored that her father felt she could run his company and had given her an actual title acknowledging that belief. She wanted nothing more than to please him.

"So what about me?" Kev asked. "What's my title? Do I get an office too?" he asked sarcastically.

The positive vibe surrounding their table quickly soured as soon as Kev spoke. Moe cleared his throat before answering.

"You won't' have an office, Kev, but you will have a corner desk in the common area while Taya and I will take the back offices. Your title will be account manager. You will help Taya. She will basically oversee the specifics of all contracts and then pass the tasks to you and the other account manager."

"Hold up, what you mean, the other account manager?" Kev asked, confused.

"I plan to hire another account manager. Business is doing great, and it will take two of you to handle the load. You will oversee the landscaping and cleaning sector of the business, while the other manager will oversee the property portion. They will handle the work orders, rent receipts, and complaints. You will send our crew out to handle cleaning jobs and landscaping jobs. You two will also work together keeping the outside of the properties maintained as well as cleaned after a move out."

"What kind of shit is that?" Kev asked,

surprising his uncle and cousin.

Moe quickly glared at his nephew silently. He was taken back by Kev's lack of appreciation. He was trying to give him a chance by even giving him a job. Not only was he not worthy of any position, Moe wasn't even confident that Kev was capable of handling the duties that came with the title.

"Come again?" Moe asked angrily. He did his best to contain his anger.

"What kind of shit is that?" he asked again. "Taya gets an office in the back with you, while as usual, I barely get shit. On top of that, you have me handling some bullshit-ass lawn jobs while you're going to hire someone from outside our family to run your properties." Kev's voice wavered between anger and hurt.

"First things first, I suggest you watch how you

talk to me. Any decision I make is for the best interest of my business. Second, you're a fucking thief, Kev. Why would I allow you to handle my properties and important shit like rent?" Moe asked, trying his best to remain calm while reasoning with his nephew.

"Man, fuck this shit. I'm out. You can keep your funky-ass job," Kev argued. "I'll find my own way. I don't want shit to do with Morgan Enterprises," he continued. Kev pushed back in his chair and stood up from the table. "Taya, I love you. Hope you enjoyed your birthday. I'ma hit you later," he said before walking off.

Moe continued to glare at Kev as they both watched him walk away. Taya wanted to call out to him, but knew that it would do no good. He was too stubborn, and to top it off he had been drinking. Moe had been raising him since he was three years old and treated him like a son until he started stealing.

Kev got outside of the restaurant and quickly walked down the street to no place in particular. He just wanted to get away from his fake-ass family. He whipped out his phone to call his niggas. He had a major proposition for them; one he knew there was no way they could refuse. And if everything worked out for him, it would be the biggest come-up in his life, and then his uncle would see who was a failure and who wasn't.

Thirteen

KEV STOOD OUTSIDE OF his homie's house and took a long swig of Hennessey straight from the top of the bottle. He swallowed the bitter liquid quickly then breathed deeply from his mouth to get rid of the foul taste stuck on his tongue. He tightened the lid back on his bottle and shoved it in the pocket of his khaki shorts. He peered down the street for a few minutes before he spotted the swift moving vehicle headed toward the house. It was Drama and Rum. It was about time. After leaving The Chateau, Kev had headed right over and had been waiting on them over a half hour. Drama and Rum pulled alongside the curb in front of the house and waved for Kev to hop in. Kev complied. The cool air in the car was welcoming in comparison to the brutal July heat outside. Before he could get comfortable in the backseat, Drama came straight with it.

"What's up nigga?" he asked curiously. "You call us out here on some urgent shit talkin' 'bout you had a major lick for us. Run it down."

"Damn!" Kev exclaimed. "I just stepped foot in this bitch."

"Well we don't have time for the pleasantries, nigga," Rum sarcastically added. "What the fuck is up? You said it was major," he added. "And it better be better than that bullshit lick we did the other night," he argued, referring to the West Side home invasion.

Kev sighed. He knew he was selling his soul to the devil for this one.

"Well as both you niggas know, my uncle is a heavy hitter out here."

"Yeah, and?" Drama asked.

"Well he's leaving the game. He's focusing on building his business and shit." He paused. "So because of this he's planning to cop his last load in a week," he said, referring to the heroin his uncle distributed in the city. Although Moe had not stated that at dinner, Kev had overheard him already making plans to pick up from Carlos the following week.

"Now, being as though him and his connect been doing business since I was a fucking lil nigga in diapers, I know he gon throw him some extra. This shipment is going to be large."

"So what the fuck that gotta do with us?" Rum asked, wondering where Kev was headed with this.

"We're going to take it," Kev stated calmly, surprising everyone.

"Wait a minute, nigga. How the fuck we gonna pull that off?" Drama asked. If it sounded too good to be true, it usually was.

"Trust me, we can pull it off and we will. You see, these niggas is old school. They have the same routine and think shit is sweet cuz they got bread. Every two weeks my dad picks up from the nigga—

right from his crib. He keeps it there because he don't gotta worry about police raiding his spot because he got a handful of those crooked-ass mufuckas in his pocket. The shipment comes in a day before my uncle actually goes and grabs it. We're going to intercept that shit before he goes and picks up. That way, we take everything that's there and we redistribute it to niggas who copping from someone else."

"How the fuck we going to get in the nigga's crib if he moving major weight like that? His shit probably tighter than Fort Knox."

"Not at all. I've been to his house numerous times. He has a bunch of niggas around during the day, but at night he relies on just his alarm system."

"That's fucking crazy!" Rum said, looking over to Drama. If what Kev was saying rang true, then their lives would change in a matter of weeks. There would be consequences behind their actions, but they weren't worried. They would handle anything that came their way, and ultimately rule the streets.

"Cool. I'm wit it," Drama stated.

"Me too," Rum agreed.

"Bet. We on that shit ASAP. I'll show you niggas where he rests, and you two lay low on the spot to become familiar."

"Nigga, we live and breathe for this shit. Just text the address," Rum stated firmly, cutting Kev off.

He wanted Kev to know he wasn't calling any shots. Never had, and never would. Drama, on the other hand, sat quietly pondering his thoughts. He wondered what made Kev come off that type of information. After all, in a way, he was crossing his uncle too. He knew Kev and his uncle Moe had that "love-hate" relationship, but he never would have thought it would come to this. He wanted to ask but figured he would do it a different way, another time. In the meantime, he would keep an eye out on Kev. If he would cross his own uncle, he would cross anyone.

* * *

The next day, Drama and Rum rode by the address Kev had provided them with to peep out the scene. Kev was right, it would be easier than taking candy from a baby. Carlos had very little security around his crib. They actually saw very little movement around the large home at all. Kev told them Carlos was very selective with his clients, but the activity around the home seemed uncharacteristically slow for a drug kingpin. They were expecting a scene more along the lines of *Scarface*, of Tony Montana stature.

"There he go again," Rum said as they watched Carlos come out of the home dressed in a black robe and slippers. He nor Drama could believe that a man of his status was so easily accessible. Money and arrogance could sure make some people stupid. Taking the binoculars from Rum, Drama looked through them. He passed them back once he too saw Carlos.

"If what Kev's saying is really true, then this could be the mother lode." Drama's excitement grew as he talked. Rum nodded in agreement. "With the work and bread we snatch outta here, we on," he added. A well-known trick in the city, he thought about all the bitches he would fuck when he came through pushing some crazy shit. Drama, on the other hand, had other plans. Since Moe was stepping down, he knew they could easily take over West Philly. However, he had no desire to run half the city with his idiot, whore-chasing cousin.

"On ain't even the word," Drama agreed. "In a few months' time, we'll be kings." He was sure of it.

Laying down the binoculars, Rum asked, "You ready to roll? We been out here for hours and this nigga ain't doing shit but taking out trash and setting out fucking dog food."

Drama agreed and they left, only to return every day for a week. For that week, nothing else mattered.

Scheming on a man like Carlos was like finding a gold mine. Kev had really come through this time.

* * *

Everything seemed to be falling in place for Trigg and Wayne. They thought they were on top of the world and nothing or no one could stop them. The both of them bought brand-new cars straight off the lot, courtesy of all the money they were bringing in due to their dope business. Moe had handed over most of the spots to them because they were making him a lot of money, and he had to show his gratitude.

They thought that everything was going smooth until some stick-up niggas kept hitting their spots. Up until now, they had no clue who was doing it. Some fiend overheard a couple of niggas talking at the poppi store, and decided to capitalize off the information. He gave it to one of Moe's people and they rewarded him with four bundles of dope.

"Yo, get Trigg on the phone and tell him to get over here. It's time for y'all niggas to prove yourselves," Moe stated.

"I'm calling him right now," replied Wayne.

"Yo, bro, I'm on my way over to the carwash on Chestnut Street if you want to meet me over there," Trigg stated, answering Wayne's call on the first ring. He was pulling his 2017 Infiniti into the lot. He had just placed some fresh new rims on it and wanted the car shining just like them.

"That can wait for another time. Right now we have another problem. The niggas that have been hitting our spots, we finally have a beat on them. Big homie wants us to roll out with him," Wayne replied.

"Word! You know what that means, right?" Trigg said, rubbing his hands together. It had been a minute since they had put in some work, and now it was about to go down. It was time to put in some work.

Fourteen

IT WAS EIGHT O'CLOCK when Kev and Drama
made it to South Philly after driving back from Jersey
where they left Rum with the work. The feds were in
the city heavy trying to crack down on all the
murders and drugs taking place. The mayor of
Philadelphia had already declared another state of
emergency. Drama had kept the plot strictly between
him and the person that really hired him. He was
grateful for Kev's assistance right now. They had left
a serious body count in SP, and between the dealers
and innocent civilians, he had already made so many
parents pull out their black dresses.

When Drama pulled onto the block, he and Kev
saw some nigga, under the hood of his F-250 Ford

pickup. They weren't even paying him any attention because he looked like he was just some smoker fixing another car.

"What's up with that fake-ass mechanic fixing your shit? Why didn't you let the shop fix it with your cheap ass?" Drama spoke in a heavy voice.

"Because I need my shit back ASAP and don't feel like waiting all day for it," Merv said.

"You got those things that I've been asking for?" Drama asked, getting straight to the point.

"Yeah, they are up in the crib. What's the problem?" Merv inquired. At the same time he received a text alert on his phone.

"I'm hearing that there's a price on those niggas who robbed big Moe's stash spots, head. Is that true?" Drama asked, trying to get some information out of him. Little did he know, he wasn't saying shit.

He was too engrossed in reading the text.

"My bad, I was trying to respond to my cousin. I have that shit in the crib if you want to grab it now," Merv recommended.

"It'd be nice, son, but you know I can't take all that dirty laundry at one time. We've been over this before," Drama retorted, knowing that if he kept the work in the same packages, it would be easy to trace back to them.

Merv's silence prompted Kev to look over at him. He saw his odd facial expression as he stood there reading another text.

"Everything cool, Merv?" Merv looked up at Kev with locked jaws and an impish look on his face. Despite his anger displaying, he was still able to keep a cool head and demeanor.

"Yeah, let's go get your shit, man, because I'm not

trying to keep that shit here anymore," Merv replied. "Then I have to go pick up my sister."

Drama quickly picked up on the throw-off, knowing that he'd just seen Na'Tae driving in her car a few minutes ago.

"Yeah, let's get that, brah," Drama said as he walked toward the house, not knowing that shit was about to get dark.

* * *

When Det. Harris received tips that something serious was about to occur in South Philly, he called his brother that worked at the First District, and also passed the info on to the feds. They were already looking for Drama and his goons.

"So tell me again. You say that this man in this photo is indeed the man that you seen killing a man at a crap game?" Agent Davis asked the informer in his office.

"Yes, I'm positive. I can't forget those features," she explained.

"Can we review the video again?" Agent Stanley asked the informer's manager.

"Come this way," the manager directed the agents. He was a tall slim black man in his fifties. He advised his employee to call the authorities when she informed him of her firsthand knowledge. When both FBI agents reviewed the tape and saw the man running away from the scene, they both smiled brightly knowing that they finally had him.

"I see why these motherfuckers always getting caught. Shit! Luck don't come no better than this," Agent Davis exclaimed while looking at the duplicate of Kev and Drama. They also had the picture of Rum.

"I'm texting my informer now, and he said to hurry up because they ready to leave."

"Tell them to chill and smoke some of that good shit that I dropped off to them to make it look real."

"Okay then, everybody get ready because it's time to take these motherfuckers away from here."

"Yes, sir," one of the other officers replied.

"Wait a minute, is that who I think it is?"

"Yes, it is, the almighty Moe," one of the other agents blurted out.

"We are about to catch two birds with one stone."

* * *

When Moe and his team pulled up the block, he could feel the temperature rising in his body telling him that something was wrong, and there was only one way to find out what it was.

"Why is it a van parked down the street, and who

the hell is in it?" Moe asked Trigg and Wayne. He knew that it could be a setup, but he really wanted to get back at those assholes for robbing his shit.

"I don't know, but I'm calling Merv's ass to find out where the hell this bitch-ass nigga is," Trigg stated. He pulled out his cellphone and dialed Merv's number. "He's not picking up!"

"Try again," Moe shouted while nonchalantly cocking his hammer.

* * *

"Please, Drama. Don't hurt him!" Smack! Drama smacked Merv's girl in the side of the face with all his force, which caused her head to smash into the headboard, which tremendously dazed her to the point that she was literally seeing innumerable stars. He again snatched the phone from her hands.

"He has thirty seconds to tell me who is trying to

set us up or you'll die with him!" Drama threatened

Gina, who didn't know what to think of the threat.

She watched Kev leave the room, this time taking

Merv's son with him.

"Please, Lord, don't let him kill my baby," Gina

softly cried out as she began praying for the safety of

herself and her son. Kev had no compassion for her

or the child, especially, after they saw that something

was a little too suspicious. That was a negative for

them both, Gina realized.

"It's my fault!" Gina cried. "I got in some trouble

and it was either I set you and your team up, or die."

"What are you talking about, set us up or die?"

Drama asked, aiming his weapon.

"I told Moe that it was y'all that robbed him, and

now he is on his way here to kill you. All he wanted

me to do was keep y'all here until he got here."

"So where the hell are they at now?" Drama asked, peeping out the window.

"I don't know, honestly. I thought they would be here by now," Gina said in a low voice. She felt defeated because she knew nothing good was about to come out of this situation. Her life was now in the hands of three cold-hearted killers.

"Thanks for the information. Your services are no longer needed," Drama whispered in her ear, then sliced her throat from ear to ear. She started gasping for air, but it was no use, as the life was leaving her body.

There was a short moment of silence before Drama spit on Gina's dead body. They knew they didn't have too much time left before they would be having company. The revelation only confirmed Drama's instincts, and once again, he would be five moves ahead of his enemies, or so he thought.

* * *

Wayne's adrenaline was running high in anticipation of laying some niggas down, and he still was moving and meticulously planning. Moe already had niggas moving into position standing on lookout. While Trigg and his team were sitting in a Chevy Malibu, they saw when Drama peeped out the window. Trigg could see the gun tucked under his shirt, and then hopped into the backseat of the black Suburban. Moe parked his Chevy Tahoe truck at the end of the block. It was 11:45 p.m., and he thoroughly searched the scenery. When he saw no threat, he emerged from the truck and then walked into the dark confines of the alley. When he walked past a couple of homeless people, he saw an old white homeless man trying to keep warm. Moe kept it moving, clutching his Glock .40 in his hands. Click! Clack!

"Put your hands in the air and turn around slowly. No stupid shit! Let's not get yourself killed," Federal Agent Davis, who Moe had just taken for a homeless man, demanded.

Not wanting to test the waters, he slowly turned around with his hands in the air. He saw the homeless man aiming a Glock 21 at him with one hand, and his credentials in the other.

"Federal agent Tod Davis."

"What the fuck!"

"And I'm federal agent Mike Stanley," the other homeless man said as he artistically cuffed Moe after taking him by surprise.

"Let me guess, you're here to kill Drama and probably Kev too, huh?" Agent Davis asked Moe while pulling the Glock from Moe's waist and inspecting it for a serial number that he knew he wouldn't find.

"No number. How many bodies?" Davis asked.

"Probably your mama and——agghh!" Moe shrilled when Davis punched him in the gut, silencing him after catching him with a TKO uppercut to his jaw line.

Moe's legs turned to jelly, but Stanley held him up. Stanley then tossed him over his shoulder and carried him into a room at the stakeout crib, which he and Davis were using as their temporary base.

Trigg was furious that Moe was not picking up the phone. He had been trying to get in touch with him to find out when they were supposed to move in. He stayed in position hoping to get the signal, while watching the entire perimeter. Trigg spotted Moe's truck but not him.

"Where the fuck is he?" Trigg said to one of his goons sitting next to him.

"He went through the alley, but we never saw him come back out. That's starting to seem a bit fishy," T-Gutta explained.

Something isn't right. Trigg instinctively felt it deep in his gut. He called Moe's phone a couple more times and got no answer. It wasn't like him to not answer, so Trigg took over and told everyone to get ready to move.

Detectives Harris and Holmes watched Trigg exit the Suburban again with the rest of his crew. There was something about the way he walked that made Holmes sense that he was packing something heavy. This man didn't give a damn about anything or body.

"Something's not right with him. Look at his

jacket," Holmes said to Harris.

They were positioned in the lot directly in front of the house where Drama and his crew were. The entire place was surrounded by undercover agents. Everyone saw it at once: the Suburban taillights illuminated and the engine started.

"He's leaving!" Holmes said into her walkie-talkie, informing Agent Davis.

"Stay on them. Matter of fact, move in now!" Then all of a sudden, she yelled, "No! No! No! 10-54 disregard!" she exclaimed over the walkie-talkie.

She saw Wayne and a couple other dudes step out of the car and walk toward the house.

"They are about to try and ambush the other suspects," Holmes informed Davis.

"Ten-four, ten-four!" Federal Agent Davis replied, highly elated and eager to take down both crews in one shot.

"Oh shit, bitch, they raiding, brah. This shit is a trap!" T-Gutta shouted as he watched the innumerable feds raid the team creeping from nowhere.

"Say what, nigga?" Wayne asked in complete shock over his phone.

He was moments away from getting on foot to go look for Moe, until he heard T-Gutta. When Trigg circled the building, he too saw the raid team with M-16 rifles and shields.

"Damn! This shit is a trap. They gotta have Moe!" Trigg exclaimed, hitting the steering wheel.

"Fall back. Man, get out of here!" he told T-Gutta as he rammed his SUV into reverse.

"I can't believe this shit, man!" Trigg said in complete disbelief, getting as far away from that place as he could. "Gina!" he shouted, after quickly putting two and two together.

The bitch pulled a snake move, Trigg thought. He couldn't wait to catch up to her so he could put a bullet through her head. Little did he know, she was already counting sheep.

Trigg couldn't believe how the FBI was everywhere. They had the place surrounded, and they had walked right into their trap. But how the fuck did anybody know? Moe wanted to know what was going on. He was left in the room with two other agents who weren't saying anything. They were only listening to the cracking of their radios and typing away on their laptops. Moe was clearly hearing the takedown of all his crew members. With his hands bound in cuffs behind his back, he couldn't do anything. It was irksome thinking of how he was going to escape from the custody of the feds. They had the gun and most likely would arrest him for it like the agent had promised, along with conspiracy to murder their fugitive. Damn it! How can life be such a bitch? Moe thought. He knew the feds didn't play fair, and he couldn't outsmart them like they had done to him and his brother. He was about to become another victim of the state, and all he wanted was to get away from these pigs. He had a daughter that would most likely end up growing up without a father figure, and would look to these crab-ass niggas in the streets to take care of her. Moe gave her everything she ever wanted, but he knew there was still one thing that he could never give her, and that was affection. She would have to look for that in another man.

He had no choice but to realize that he might be facing reality. He couldn't imagine being behind another prison wall. Moe always told himself that the only way he would ever get caught is if they carried him out in a body bag, but the thought of his daughter changed all that. He decided to let the chips fall where they may. As a man, he was going take this shit on the chin and hopefully get off. Besides they still didn't say what they were holding him for. In fact, they never even read him his Miranda rights. This was his key to getting all the charges dropped. He just smiled and sat there, patiently awaiting the outcome of everything.

Fifteen

FEDERAL AGENT DAVIS CONTINUED the raid on Drama's crew. Wayne and T-Gutter were both armed with AR-15s and M-16 rifles with silencers on them to muffle the sound. They slowly crept up on the four agents guarding the back of the home. Per routine, Davis stopped short of the door as he carefully and instinctively listened. He heard what sounded like a game being play on a loud television set. Kicking down the door and not knowing where anybody was, was Davis's only fear, because he or one of his men would be in the line of fire. He waved the two men operating the battering ram around him, and they stood prepared in front of the door.

"1652. All power now!" Davis said into his earpiece.

"Ten-four," the agent answered. A second later, all power in the building was shut down. Lord, here it goes! Davis thought. Detectives Harris and Holmes watched the raid from a distance. At a finger snap from Davis, the door came down with the battering ram, followed by two M84 flashbang grenades.

Boom! Boom!

"Federal agents, get—!"

Boom! Boom! Boom!

Before Davis could complete his orders, shots were fired. Kev shot the first agent that came through the door then turned his gun on the other agents while they watched their fellow officer hit the ground. He backed himself near the bathroom while squeezing his Glock .45. Drama attempted to hold his ground, firing wildly at the agents, but he had been blinded by the flashbang and was taken down by a single shot to the forehead from Agent Davis.

Once the gunshots started, Wayne and his crew started dropping the feds posted up outside like dominos. Trigg snuck over to the house where Moe was being held and peeped through the window. All he could see was the two agents yelling through their mics, trying to make sure their friends were okay. He quickly made his way around to the entrance, trying not to be spotted. There were agents and regular cops on the scene, and mayhem had erupted.

Once he made it inside, he hit the first agent with a single round, right between the eyes. He was dead before he hit the ground. The other agent tried to get a shot off in his direction, but Moe was too fast for him. He jumped up and rammed his shoulder into the agent sending him flying against the glass table. With precision, Trigg fired two rounds in his direction. The first one missed, but the second one found its mark, hitting the agent dead in the neck.

"Let's get the duck out of here now," Moe yelled.

They ran through the house trying to find a way out. When they made it to the back door, Wayne and his team had already cleared out all the agents that were out there, giving Trigg and Moe a path to escape. As they made it to the car, Moe spotted Kev trying to creep one of his young bulls. He ran over and punched him in the back of his head, making him drop his gun. Moe kicked him in the stomach and stumped on his leg.

Kev attempted to go for his MAC-10 that was resting on the floor a few feet away from him. However, Moe popped him twice in his gut with the Glock .40 that Trigg tossed him. Then rocking him to sleep, he squeezed two more slugs into his thighs, making him suffer a little. On the living room floor, imbruing the snow-white carpet with the blood pouring from his gut, Kev knew that he was on borrowed time until death came upon him.

"Man, I thought we were family!" Kev winced in devastating pain while crawling away from Moe and Trigg, dragging his lower body.

"Man, fuck family, this right here is my family,

nigga," Moe replied, pointing at Trigg. "He was the one who came to save me when everyone else left me for dead."

"That nigga is not your family," Kev said in pain.

"What? Man, fuck you, bitch-ass nigga."

"No, fuck you, pussy," Drama said, then spit in their direction, missing them both.

BOOM! BOOM! BOOM! BOCA! BOCA! BOCA! BOCA!

"For the deadly sin you've committed in the mafia's name," Moe said as him and Trigg rushed out of there trying to get away.

Boom! Boom! Boom! Boom!

"You go that way and we'll meet up later. Watch yourself lil homie, and thanks," Moe said, dapping Trigg up.

"I hope Wayne got away," Trigg said as he ran in the opposite direction.

When he reached the corner, he turned around

just in time to see the cops surrounding Moe. He didn't have his hands in the air, so Trigg knew what was about to go down. He wouldn't be able to stop it if he tried. A hail of gunfire broke out, and Trigg could see Moe falling face-first to the ground. Trigg didn't even shed a tear; his heart went cold, and his eyes turned black. His mentor and boss was gone to the world forever.

"Goodbye, big homie," he said, turning around and running away from the scene. As he ran down the street, a car pulled alongside him. Thinking that it was the feds, Trigg turned around with his gun ready to go off. He stopped when he saw familiar faces. It was Na'Tae and Wayne. Trigg jumped in the car and they sped off.

As they drove away from the bloody murder scene, Trigg and Wayne both sat in silence thinking about what just took place and what their lives would be like if they stayed in this business. Trigg just wanted his family back and to live like a normal teenage kid, having fun in college somewhere. He decided that this was it for him. He was officially out of the game. He was going to move out of Philly and start rebuilding his family with his best friend and brother from another mother Wayne, and his soon to be wife, Na'Tae.

When they pulled into a deserted gas station, Na'Tae got out to stretch her legs. Wayne stepped out to make a call while Trigg was leaned back in his seat with his eyes closed. He quickly jumped up when he felt cold steel on his forehead.

"Don't move, nigga."

When he looked up at who was holding the gun, he couldn't believe it. Wayne had a smirk on his face and greed in his eyes.

"So this is how it is, huh? You set all this shit up so that you could run shit. I would have given everything to you, bro. I was getting out of the game."

"Fuck you, nigga! I'm going to make sure that you get out and never come back. Everybody always looked at me as the weakest link, but not no more. Goodbye, bro," Wayne said, about to squeeze the trigger.

BOCA! BOCA!

Trigg looked up and Na'Tae was holding her 9 mm in hand. Wayne was squirming in pain as she walked up on him.

"I knew this nigga wasn't right, baby."

Wayne knew he was about to die, so he started spitting and cursing like there was no tomorrow. It definitely wouldn't be for him. He was being so disrespectful that Trigg couldn't believe that it was his own peoples talking like that. He stepped out of the car, and him and Na'Tae aimed at Wayne, who was continuing to talk crazy. Before Wayne could finish his disrespect toward Trigg and his family, they both emptied their clips into his face, leaving him deformed in a gruesome splatter of blood and brains. They then hopped back in the car and inconspicuously left the scene. Na'Tae then took I-95 south all the way to Miami and met up with her peoples, who would help them clean their dirty money and start a new life together . . .

Text Good2Go at 31996 to receive new release updates via text message

To order books, please fill out the order form below:
To order films please go to www.good2gofilms.com

Name:_____

Address:_____

City: _____ State: _____ Zip Code: _____

Phone:_____

Email:_____

Method of Payment: Check   VISA   MASTERCARD

Credit Card#:_____

Name as it appears on card: _____

Signature: _____

Item Name	Price	Qty	Amount
48 Hours to Die – Silk White	$14.99		
A Hustler's Dream - Ernest Morris	$14.99		
A Hustler's Dream 2 - Ernest Morris	$14.99		
Black Reign – Ernest Morris	$14.99		
Bloody Mayhem Down South	$14.99		
Business Is Business – Silk White	$14.99		
Business Is Business 2 – Silk White	$14.99		
Business Is Business 3 – Silk White	$14.99		
Childhood Sweethearts – Jacob Spears	$14.99		
Childhood Sweethearts 2 – Jacob Spears	$14.99		
Childhood Sweethearts 3 - Jacob Spears	$14.99		
Childhood Sweethearts 4 - Jacob Spears	$14.99		
Connected To The Plug – Dwan Marquis Williams	$14.99		
Connected To The Plug 2 – Dwan Marquis Williams	$14.99		
Deadly Reunion – Ernest Morris	$14.99		
Flipping Numbers – Ernest Morris	$14.99		
Flipping Numbers 2 – Ernest Morris	$14.99		
He Loves Me, He Loves You Not - Mychea	$14.99		
He Loves Me, He Loves You Not 2 - Mychea	$14.99		
He Loves Me, He Loves You Not 3 - Mychea	$14.99		
He Loves Me, He Loves You Not 4 – Mychea	$14.99		
He Loves Me, He Loves You Not 5 – Mychea	$14.99		
Lord of My Land – Jay Morrison	$14.99		
Lost and Turned Out – Ernest Morris	$14.99		
Married To Da Streets – Silk White	$14.99		
M.E.R.C. - Make Every Rep Count Health and Fitness	$14.99		

Money Make Me Cum – Ernest Morris	$14.99		
My Besties – Asia Hill	$14.99		
My Besties 2 – Asia Hill	$14.99		
My Besties 3 – Asia Hill	$14.99		
My Besties 4 – Asia Hill	$14.99		
My Boyfriend's Wife - Mychea	$14.99		
My Boyfriend's Wife 2 – Mychea	$14.99		
My Brothers Envy – J. L. Rose	$14.99		
My Brothers Envy 2 – J. L. Rose	$14.99		
Naughty Housewives – Ernest Morris	$14.99		
Naughty Housewives 2 – Ernest Morris	$14.99		
Naughty Housewives 3 – Ernest Morris	$14.99		
Naughty Housewives 4 – Ernest Morris	$14.99		
Never Be The Same – Silk White	$14.99		
Stranded – Silk White	$14.99		
Slumped – Jason Brent	$14.99		
Supreme & Justice – Ernest Morris	$14.99		
Tears of a Hustler - Silk White	$14.99		
Tears of a Hustler 2 - Silk White	$14.99		
Tears of a Hustler 3 - Silk White	$14.99		
Tears of a Hustler 4- Silk White	$14.99		
Tears of a Hustler 5 – Silk White	$14.99		
Tears of a Hustler 6 – Silk White	$14.99		
The Panty Ripper - Reality Way	$14.99		
The Panty Ripper 3 – Reality Way	$14.99		
The Solution – Jay Morrison	$14.99		
The Teflon Queen – Silk White	$14.99		
The Teflon Queen 2 – Silk White	$14.99		
The Teflon Queen 3 – Silk White	$14.99		
The Teflon Queen 4 – Silk White	$14.99		
The Teflon Queen 5 – Silk White	$14.99		
The Teflon Queen 6 - Silk White	$14.99		
The Vacation – Silk White	$14.99		
Tied To A Boss - J.L. Rose	$14.99		

BLACK REIGN

Tied To A Boss 2 - J.L. Rose	$14.99		
Tied To A Boss 3 - J.L. Rose	$14.99		
Tied To A Boss 4 - J.L. Rose	$14.99		
Tied To A Boss 5 - J.L. Rose	$14.99		
Time Is Money - Silk White	$14.99		
Tomorrow's Not Promised	$14.99		
Two Mask One Heart – Jacob Spears and Trayvon Jackson	$14.99		
Two Mask One Heart 2 – Jacob Spears and Trayvon Jackson	$14.99		
Two Mask One Heart 3 – Jacob Spears and Trayvon Jackson	$14.99		
Wrong Place Wrong Time – Silk White	$14.99		
Young Goonz – Reality Way	$14.99		
Subtotal:			
Tax:			
Shipping (Free) U.S. Media Mail:			
Total:			

Make Checks Payable To:
Good2Go Publishing
7311 W Glass Lane,
Laveen, AZ 85339

CPSIA information can be obtained
at www.ICGtesting.com
Printed in the USA
LVOW10s1808031117
554902LV00010B/619/P